THE Archie® ENCYCLOPEDIA

SCRIPT
Jamie Lee Rotante
Ian Flynn
Caty Koehl
Gillian Swearingen

EDITOR-IN-CHIEF/PRESIDENT
Mike Pellerito

PUBLISHER
Jon Goldwater

COVER
Dan Parent

BOOK DESIGN
Vincent Lovallo

SPECIAL THANKS
Kari McLachlan

SENIOR DIRECTOR OF EDITORIAL
Jamie Lee Rotante

EDITORIAL TEAM
Vincent Lovallo
Stephen Oswald

FEATURING THE TALENTS OF:
Dan Parent, Andrew Pepoy, Andy Fish, Art Baltazar, Audrey Mok,
Bill Galvan, Bill Golliher, Bill Vigoda, Bill Woggin, Bob Bolling, Bob Smith,
Bob White, Brittney Williams, Cameron Stewart, Chris Lie, Craig Cermak,
Dan DeCarlo, Derek Charm, Stephanie Coronado, Ed Fagaly, Eva Cabrera,
Fernando Ruiz, Fiona Staples, Francesco Francavilla, Franco, Gisele Lagace,
Glenn Whitmore, Harry Lucey, Henry Scarpelli, J Bone, Jason Jensen,
Jeff Shultz, Joe Edwards, Joe Eisma, Joe Staton, John Lucas, Jon D'Agostino,
Kelly Fitzpatrick, Kelsey Shannon, Laura Braga, Margeruite Sauvage,
Mark McNabb, Matt Herms, Michael Walsh, Mike Allred, Norm Breyfogle,
Orlando Busino, Pat Kennedy, Tim Kennedy, Pete Woods, Peter Krause,
Rex Lindsey, Rick Burchette, Rick Koslowski, Robert Hack, Rudy Lapick,
Ryan Jampole, Samm Schwartz, Sandy Jarrell, Stan Goldberg, Steven Butler,
Terry Austin, Thomas Pitilli, Rosario "Tito" Peña, Tod Smith, Tracy Yardley,
Tyra White Meadows, Veronica Fish, Vincent Lovallo

TABLE OF CONTENTS

INTRODUCTION

Welcome to the expanded, extensive, and entertaining world of Archie Comics! If you're new here, this is the perfect starting point for any to-be fans. We've got a comprehensive overview of almost every single Archie character that's existed—for now— plus some notable furry friends, notable locations, and essential items. If you're already a fan? Then you're going to love this guide to all the characters and worlds you know and love, and maybe even a few you've never heard of before!

The cast of Archie characters is vast, many of which haven't been seen in years—but we've done our best to unearth every one we could find. This is the ultimate who's who (as well as what's what) of the Archieverse.

So, are you ready to learn all there is to learn about the World of Archie? Turn the page and let's begin!

WELCOME TO RIVERDALE!

Ah, Riverdale, home sweet home to Archie and all of his friends, foes, and family! Riverdale has always been a welcoming place to all its citizens—except, you know, when zombie hordes, vampires, and other various monsters and paranormal entities take over. Even then, its people know to take care of one another above all else.

In this section, we're going to focus on the various residents, shopkeepers, and transplants in Riverdale throughout its history. From Riverdale High School to Riverdale in the year 3000, you'll meet all the teens, their families, various students and faculty, and noteworthy local heroes in America's favorite hometown!

ARCHIE ANDREWS

First Appearance: *Pep Comics #22*, 1941

Hair: Red (well, more so orange)

Eyes: Blue

Hobbies: Football, basketball, baseball, hockey, skateboarding, going on dates, doing everything he can to stay on Mr. Lodge's good side (no one said you have to be "good" at a hobby!)

Likes: Girls, milkshakes, girls, sports, girls, going to the beach (to see more girls!)

Dislikes: Homework, shoveling snow, Reggie's pranks

Originally known as "America's Typical Teenager," Archie Andrews has become the most lovable kid in town and is anything but typical! His signature cross-cut red hair and freckles paint the perfect portrait of Archie's klutzy-but-kind nature. He is always willing to help out friends and hopes to lead his band The Archies to the top of the charts!

While not a straight-A student, what Arch lacks in academic ability he makes up for in the romance department—namely his relationships with Betty and Veronica! The best friends tend to fight over the redheaded Romeo… although Archie is notorious for keeping both in a never-ending love triangle!

He is not just a teenage Casanova though–Archie has a reputation of being selfless, loyal, and someone who is eager to lend a hand anytime. Archie is respectful of authority, but somehow is always in trouble, particularly with his high school principal,, Mr. Weatherbee. Likewise, Veronica's father, Hiram Lodge, is usually visibly shaken when he sees Archie entering his mansion.

DID YOU KNOW?

- It is believed that the character of Archie was based on the immensely popular *Andy Hardy* movies of the 1930s, starring Mickey Rooney (kids, ask your grandparents who that is!).

- True to his Scottish roots, Archie can play the bagpipes!

- Archie really isn't all that clumsy. He's actually quite nimble on his feet—he just doesn't want other people to know that or he'd become TOO popular!

THE Archies ®

Archie is the lead singer of his own band—The Archies (what he lacks in band naming skills he makes up for in musical ability!). The band made its first debut in *Life with Archie* #60, published in April 1967. The fictional band was inspired by the success of the 1966 TV series *The Monkees*.

Dan Parent

The Archies play a variety of contemporary popular music, usually reflective of the time the whatever comic they're featured in comes out. Every member sings vocals, but each member has a specific role as well. Archie handles lead guitar and vocals.

As band leader, Archie takes his art seriously, never missing a practice, and can often be found with his guitar slung over his shoulder. He spends much of his free time coming up with lyrics and melodies.

Archie

FRESHMAN YEAR

Archie's been in high school for over 80 years—but he didn't just jump to his junior year without going through the trials and tribulations of being a freshman! In a series published in 2009, Archie entered Riverdale High School with big dreams of the future—what he didn't expect was having to confront the reality of his best friend moving away, schoolwork piling up, and dealing with everyone's least favorite part of freshman year: bullies. Archie handled it all in stride and made the most out of this time thanks to his compassion and courage… and a few detentions along the way!

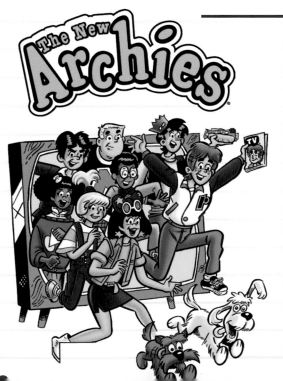

The New Archies

We couldn't possibly have a little Archie and a pre-teen Archie without also seeing Archie in middle school. Ah, middle school—a time that's awkward for everyone, complete with unfortunate haircuts and growth spurts—something even Archie Andrews couldn't escape! In the early 1990s, there was a radical redesign of the Little Archie universe. Renamed *The New Archies*, the formerly "Little" Archie now had some hip threads, went on goofy adventures, and sported very stylish mullet (well, as stylish as one can be!).

little Archie
and his pals

Before Archie became an effortlessly cool teenager, he was a little kid with a thirst for adventure! Little Archie made his first comic book appearance in his very own series in 1956. The world of Little Archie is very similar to that of his teenage counterpart—though it often incorporates aspects of adventure, sci-fi, and even some horror (ok, I guess it really is like teen Archie's world!). Most of the same characters are featured, albeit usually in younger versions. Little Archie is tenacious, curious, and is always willing to help out those in need—and eager to always learn about the world around him!

WORLDS OF ARCHIE

PUREHEART THE POWERFUL™

When we say that Archie is anything but typical, we mean it! Archie may be a mild-mannered teen, but when he attempted to tap into the "PH Factor," a superpower only accessed by those pure of heart, he became a crimefighting superhero! Archie first acquired these super abilities in *Life with Archie* #42, published in 1965. Pureheart is super-strong, super-resilient, and can fly using his "jet-boosters." However, his powers only exist as long as his heart is pure, leading to embarrassing situations such as him losing his powers after an appreciative kiss from a damsel in distress... a pretty big weakness for a guy with two girlfriends!

From super heroics to super spy, Archie branched into the high-tech world of secret agents with a series that started as a parody of 1960s spy shows (namely *The Man from U.N.C.L.E.*). Archie first appeared as the Man from R.I.V.E.R.D.A.L.E. in *Life with Archie* #45, with Archie as a spy working with world defense organization P.O.P. (an acronym for Protect our Planet). Their chief enemy is a counter-group known as C.R.U.S.H. (a spoof on THRUSH, but whose acronym was never explained). R.I.V.E.R.D.A.L.E. stands for Really Impressive Vast Enterprise for Routing Dangerous Adversaries, Louts,

Etc. *The Man from R.I.V.E.R.D.A.L.E.* series made a cameo in a 2008 issue of *Archie* and was revived for a four-part series in the same title in 2010. The Man from R.I.V.E.R.D.A.L.E. returned in *Jughead* #3 in February 2016.

Archie's EXPLORERS OF THE UNKNOWN!

REX W. LINDSEY

AN ACTION PACKED ADVENTURE BEGINS

Archie also got into the explorer spirit when he became "Red" Andrews, a Soldier of Fortune as part of *Archie's Explorers of the Unknown*—a short-lived series that began in 1990. Explorers of the Unknown was a parody of Jack Kirby's *Challengers of the Unknown*, and Archie and friends were an elite group of adventurers who were dispatched to combat mad villains and explore uncharted areas.

Archie even dabbled in some detective work. As reporter for the Riverdale High school newspaper, he took to solving both standard and strange occurrences around town… or as we like to call them: WEIRD MYSTERIES! A 1999 series, aptly titled *Archie's Weird Mysteries*, was based on an animated TV series of the same name, which saw Archie heroically come face-to-face with the likes of vampires, UFOs, giant insects, and even a tapioca pudding glob! (Just your standard small-town fare!)

Archie's WEIRD MYSTERIES

ARCHIE THROUGHOUT TIME

Thanks to the wonders of comic book science, Archie has not only been able to be a teenager for 80 years, he's also lived both in prehistoric times and 1,000 years into the future! In Archie 1, which first started in *Life with Archie* #81 published in 1969, the ancestors of Archie and the gang live as cavemen, interacting with dinosaurs and other prehistoric beasts. Along with his friends, Archie makes discoveries like the first ever Christmas celebration, fire, wheels, and more!

Then, we zoom into the far future— the year 3000, to be exact!—with Archie's descendants, who live in an technologically advanced Riverdale, complete with flying cars, moving sidewalks, and robots to boot! But even in the future, Archie still isn't immune to dating drama, running late to school, or awkward mullet haircuts!

Traveling through time can be serious business, too. In *Archie: 1941*, a mini-series originally published in 2018, Archie Andrews graduated Riverdale High and found himself torn between going to college or getting a job. But all of his plans changed when the United States made its entrance into World War II. Archie makes the ultimate decision to enlist in the armed forces and is deployed to North Africa, while many of his friends and family back in Riverdale try to get by knowing that their beloved friend and son is laying his life on the line for the good of his country.

In the same vein as *Archie: 1941*, *Archie: 1955*, originally published in 2019, places Archie right at the dawn of rock 'n' roll, acting as a surrogate Elvis Presley! Tired of making the same old music in the sleepy little town of Riverdale, Archie and his bandmates decided to shake things up and bring a little Rock 'n' Roll to their school dance. Their musical stunt caught the attention of music mogul Rick Sterling. He became famous so quickly that he ended up on national television in no time. Archie soon fell to the pressure of becoming a celebrity. Much to his surprise, he learned that being the center of attention came with a loss of autonomy. This ordeal changed his life and also his attitude—leading him to realize what was most important to him in life.

ARCHIE MEETS...

Archie might just be the luckiest guy alive—especially with the sheer numbers of celebrities and star power he's crossed paths with! In his history, Archie, as well as his band, have rubbed elbows with some of the biggest names in music, film, and sports!

A few notable visitors to Riverdale include: legendary rock band KISS, football Hall of Famer and TV personality Michael Strahan, iconic punk bands like The Ramones and Blondie, actor and activist George Takei, superstar singer Lady Gaga, Facebook creator Mark Zuckerberg, and even fellow TV band celebrities The Monkees— and that's only naming a few!

Plus, Riverdale has been greeted by the likes of some real out-of-this-world characters, like the Punisher, Predator, and even a once-in-a-lifetime encounter with a Sharknado!

…Okay we may have spoke too soon in regards to Archie's "luck," not everything has been rainbows and sunshine in the world of Riverdale—and that was especially true in October 2013, when Archie found himself smack dab in the middle of a zombie apocalypse that touched down in Riverdale.

When the zombies take over, Archie and those closest to him are forced to flee the place they call home. As one of the refugee leaders, he tries to hang onto his idealism and humanity.

RIVERDALE

Archie got the biggest makeover in his history when he got a live-action counterpart thanks to the wildly successful CW TV series *Riverdale*! Archie, played by KJ Apa, is a star football player with a passion for writing and playing music. He's always trying to do what's best for his friends, his family, and his town. Once again tackling the more serious (and occasionally darker) side of life, Archie is an intense and conflicted teenager who wears his heart on his sleeve. That being said, he still knows how to hold his own when he's faced with conflict and is both tough and athletic—being a star on the football team as well as a trained boxer. Archie is loyal to a fault and will put everything on the line to protect his amily and friends.

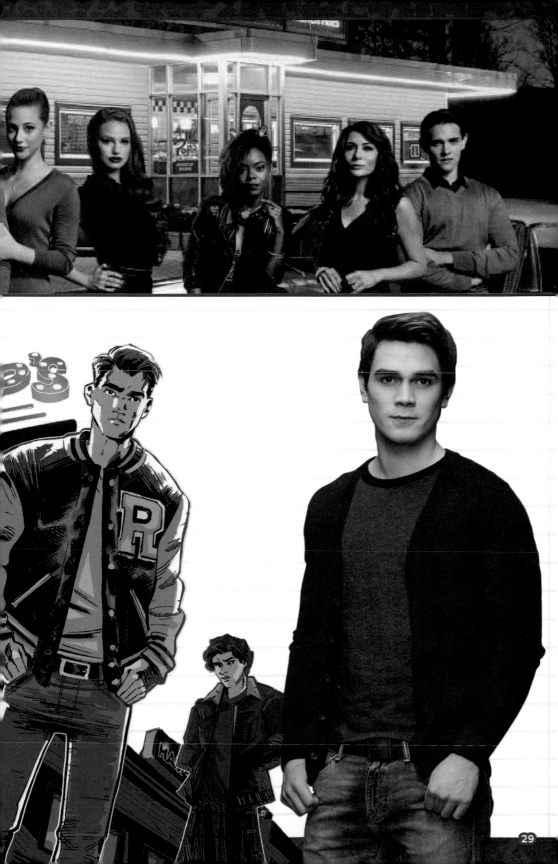

THE LOVE TRIANGLE

Synonymous with Archie is that of the famed Love Triangle that exists between himself, Betty Cooper, and Veronica Lodge. Betty Cooper made her first appearance in the comics at the same time Archie did, in *Pep Comics* #22, 1941, quickly establishing herself as the girl-next-door who Archie tried his best to impress. Veronica Lodge arrived on the scene four issues later (*Pep Comics* #26, 1941) as the new, intriguing girl in Riverdale.

The two potential love interests have carried stories for the decades since they were established. Sometimes, Archie prefers Veronica, with Betty acting as a back-up option. Other times, Betty is the chosen over high-maintenance Veronica. Most of the time, though, Archie can't make his mind up at all! Betty and Veronica pursue their mutual love interest in kind, too, using their own methods to catch his attention, often leading them to sabotage one another. Despite this, the two maintain a friendship!

Archie was forced to finally make a choice in a special four-part storyline called "Love Showdown" that started in *Archie* #429, in 1994—much to everyone's dismay, he actually chose the fiery red-headed Cheryl Blossom! However, a sequel soon returned the love triangle to its status quo.

Another major shakeup happened in *Archie* #600 in 2009, which saw Archie propose to Veronica! In subsequent issues, the two planned a wedding and welcomed a beautiful set of twins. Then in issue #603 Archie proposed to and married Betty! While this is revealed to have been a fantasy triggered by walking down Riverdale's Memory Lane, it started the trend of giving a peek into the future and Archie's separate lives married to Betty and Veronica. More on that next...

LIFE WITH Archie

The history-making *Life with Archie* series (2010-2014) followed the parallel universes of Archie's married lives with both Betty and Veronica. In the Archie Loves Veronica universe, Archie and Veronica's marriage was off to a rocky start thanks to Archie's father-in-law and boss Hiram Lodge. Things got so tough Archie and Veronica ended up separating—until a mine collapse that awakened Archie to the reality of multiple universes changed his life and made Veronica realize just how much she still cared for him.

Things in Archie's married life with Betty weren't exactly easy, either. After a tumultuous start in NYC with Archie's lackluster musical career, the two decided to move back home to Riverdale and both took on teaching positions at Riverdale High! Archie also took on the job of opening a restaurant with childhood friends Jughead and Ambrose while still teaching and coaching his music students after school. When Betty gets promoted to Assistant Principal, it gets even more trying for the two of them to dedicate time to each other—which led Archie to question their marriage and where it was going.

Ultimately, Archie was able to salvage his marriages in both worlds—but one thing also became true in both: he ended up sacrificing his life to save his friend Kevin Keller's, cementing him forever as Riverdale's own homegrown hero.

BETTY COOPER

First Appearance: *Pep Comics #22, 1941*

Hair: Blonde

Eyes: Blue

Hobbies: Volunteer work, babysitting, fixing old cars, softball, scuba diving, studying

Likes: Reading, writing, community justice, Archie!

Dislikes: Arguments, injustice, coming in second place

Confident and caring, Elizabeth "Betty" Cooper is the classic girl-next-door. Her sweet nature makes her one of the friendliest gals around. Betty is an avid writer who never goes a day without filling her diary with thoughts and stories. Her entries usually focus on a day in Riverdale High, but occasionally these tales can become fantastical sagas starring her fellow students! She hopes to one day showcase her work and become a famous author.

Betty's kindhearted ways have endeared her to everyone in Riverdale. She's always ready to help out those who are in need—whether it's volunteering at the hospital or fixing up Archie's broken-down jalopy. She excels in school, sports, and extracurricular activities—everything except for romance, where she often finds herself playing second fiddle to her BFF Veronica Lodge for Archie's undivided attention. She never lets this get her down though, and her kindhearted ways have endeared her to everyone in Riverdale.

DID YOU KNOW?

- Betty's got plenty of musical skills. She can play guitar, tambourine, the recorder, maracas, banjo, keyboard, saxophone, cello, and the bongos!

- Betty's the leader of the Green Girls, formerly the Goodwill Girls: a group of like-minded teens who gather together to do volunteer work for the environment and their community.

- Betty's ponytail is removable and controls her every action because she's actually an alien—wait, that was only in a "what if" story, not actually true! Sorry about that!

THE Archies

Betty is the lead guitarist, percussionist, and one of the three singers of The Archies. Originally, in addition to singing Betty also played the tambourine. But Betty's not just a background player in the band—in fact, she loves writing music (especially lyrics!) just as much as Archie does!

Similar to writing in her diary, Betty uses lyrics as a way to express everything that's going on in her life and in her head. While her drive, determination, and focus on practicing and contributing to making The Archies the best they can be is paramount, Betty also secretly dreams of breaking off and pursuing a solo career as a singer-songwriter, joining the ranks of women before her like Joni Mitchell, Fiona Apple, and Taylor Swift.

little Archie and his pals

Even from a young age Betty was strong-willed and determined, and excelled at any sports she played! She accompanied Little Archie many times on some of his adventures, holding her own in some thrilling and scary experiences they both shared; occasionally the two would also be joined by Little Archie's dog Spotty and Little Betty's kitten Caramel.

Little Betty would often try her hardest to spend as much time with Little Archie as she could, be it walking home from school with him or doing his homework, even if it meant getting herself in trouble so she could have detention with him!

Despite the special moments she shared with Little Archie during these years, she still often found herself coming in second to Little Veronica!

Archie

FRESHMAN YEAR

Betty approached her freshman year at Riverdale High School head-first, determined to move on from Archie and not get so hung up on getting him to like her back... or at least that was what she thought. She was also not going to let Veronica undermine her or look down on her because of her clothing or attitude—she was going to show Veronica that she could be just as stylish and headstrong as her BFF and get Archie's attention in the process! Of course, that attitude didn't last long—she could never truly let Archie come between her and her friendship with Veronica!

The New Archies

Betty's ponytail got a lift and she sported some fun pink overalls in *The New Archies*—which was one of the less wild character appearance changes that took place! In this series, Betty was a timid preteen who was, of course, hopelessly in love with young Archie Andrews. While often times shy and nervous around others, Betty was still eager to help out her friends—even if it meant going toe-to-toe with neighborhood bullies!

WORLDS OF BETTY

SUPERTEEN ™

Betty also got the superhero
treatment when she became Superteen in
Betty & Veronica #118 (1965)! Sporting a
blue cape and tights, Superteen has the
powers of flight, resilience, and super-
strength, and can access these powers
with just a twist of her magic ponytail!
While her powers may seem similar to
Pureheart's, there's one big difference: his
are limited and dependent on keeping his
heart pure. Superteen has control of her
powers and uses this to uplift the rest of
her team. One could argue that she's the
real hero of the Super Teens (it's probably
why they're named after her!).

Archie's EXPLORERS OF THE UNKNOWN! ™

A real gadget-gal, in *Explorers
of the Unknown*, Betty went by
the moniker of Wheels Cooper,
where she was the head
mechanic and pilot—bringing
her teen world skills of auto work
together with a new ability to
pilot any sort of transportation,
be it helicopter or submarine!

Betty Cooper is Riverdale's number one (sharing the spot, as always, with Veronica) Scream Queen in Riverdale when Weird Mysteries abound! And who could blame her? Especially when it came to dealing with haunted nightmares, killer bees, and pirate ghouls! But that doesn't mean Betty's a coward—she's so tough she even channeled Lara Croft and battled against a practical joke demon that wreaked havoc on Riverdale!

SPY GIRLZ

Mild-mannered teen by day, spies by night! In a story that began in *Betty & Veronica Spectacular* #87 (2009), Betty Cooper (along with BFF Veronica Lodge) lives an undercover life of a secret agent, fighting for truth, justice, and the Riverdale way! Going by the alias "Agent B," Betty prefers to play the role of good cop, and despite her athletic abilities and high-tech gear, she prefers relying on good-old fashioned conversation (along with her handy dandy lie detector and decoder watch) to uncover the truth!

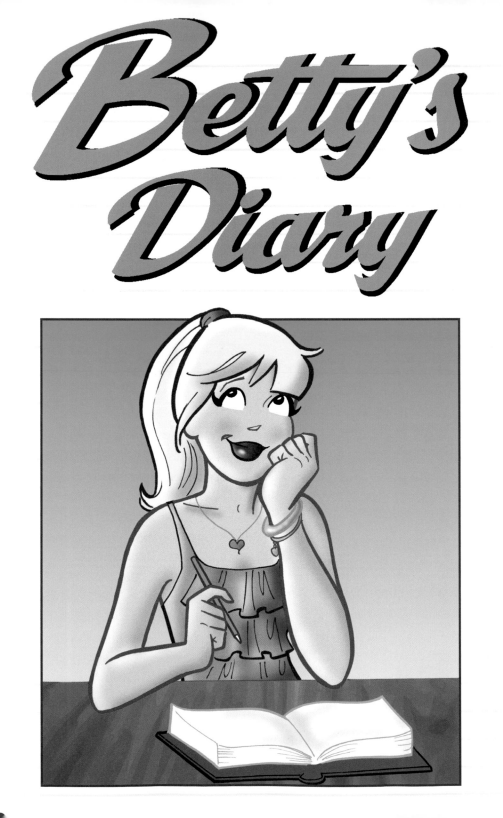

By now we all know that Betty enjoys writing and keeps a diary—but that's so well-known in Riverdale that she even had her own series dedicated to her diary entries! Starting in 1986, *Betty's Diary* detailed the ins and outs of Betty's life, exploring her dreams and even some of the struggles she faced at school and at home. Ever a journalist-in-training, Betty wrote down nearly every important event which occurred in her life, and kept it under lock-and-key in her precious journal; stories involving romance, adventure, and betrayal.

We got yet another peek at Betty's not-so-secret diary in the 2014 novel *Diary of a Girl Next Door: Betty*. In this special book Betty was once again transported back to her freshman year of high school. On top of being a nervous freshman, she also dealt with major drama involving her best friend Veronica, overcoming mountains of homework, and surviving the everyday rigors of high school!

Don't be fooled by Betty's sweet demeanor—she's not a pushover! This is especially true in the Archie Horror line. In *Afterlife with Archie*, Betty isn't afraid to stand up for herself—whether that's against Veronica or a horde of ravenous zombies. It was her steadfast and compassionate nature that endeared her so much to Archie, he actually proposed to her!

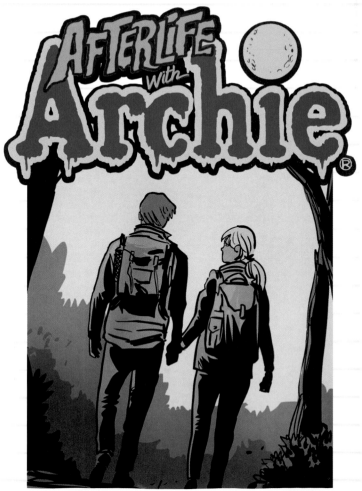

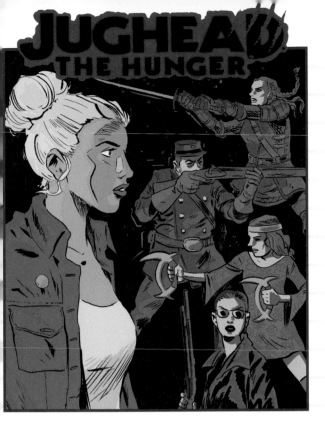

In *Jughead: The Hunger*, Betty is a legacy werewolf hunter, hailing from a long-line of werewolf hunters that have always taken down Jughead's family of werewolves (don't worry, you'll find out more on that later!). Betty befriended Archie and faked her affections towards him in an effort to get closer to the newest werewolf of Riverdale, Jughead. However, she eventually grew to care about Jughead and his family. She found herself torn between loyalties to her friends, her family, and her duty to protect the town.

Betty & Veronica Vixens

Don't believe yet that Betty Cooper is fierce? Maybe you will when you see her leading a biker gang! Along with Veronica, she started up the Vixens, a group of teen girls determined to oust the villainous Southside Serpent gang (more on them later, too!) and restore order in Riverdale. Tired of sitting behind Archie on his motorcycle, Betty fixed up her dad's old bike, learned how to ride it, and set off on showing just how much butt the girls in Riverdale can kick when they're messed with!

RIVERDALE

Betty, played by Lili Reinhart, is shy and mild-mannered. However, she's always willing to fight for what's right, especially when it comes to people she cares about. Betty is a straight-A student and arguably one of the most intelligent students at Riverdale High School.

Ever the overachiever, Betty strives to be the perfect student, daughter, and sister. Many view her as the perfect girl-next-door, but that couldn't be farther from the truth. Betty suffers from anger and aggression issues, often resulting in her clenching her fist so intensely that she leaves scars on her palms.

Betty is also prone to losing control and channeling a darker side of herself. In spite of this, she is still a loving person that people love to have at their side.

Betty also shows a great deal of strength, courage, and nerve. She is constantly fighting for her friends and family and will do whatever it takes to defend her loved ones, even if it means making some impulsive decisions. However, she isn't afraid to stand her ground and stand up for herself. A child of two journalists, Betty has developed formidable sleuthing skills and an unyielding dedication to finding out the truth at any cost.

VERONICA LODGE

Name: Veronica "Ronnie" Lodge

First Appearance: *Pep Comics #26,* April 1942

Hair: Blue-Black

Eyes: Brown

Hobbies: Shopping, investing, girlbossing

Likes: New clothes smell, fashion, shopping, being the center of attention

Dislikes: Slobs, being ignored, having her credit cards deactivated

Known as Riverdale's privileged princess, Veronica Lodge is the richest gal in town. Not a lifelong Rivedaler (Riverdalian? Riverdalite?), Veronica and her family moved there and immediately took the entire town by storm. She comes from big money, thanks to her tycoon father Hiram Lodge. She tends to focus on the finer things in life, from the fanciest threads to the most exclusive restaurants, and has no issue waving her money around for the world to see!

"Ronnie" also has a habit of using her wealth to snag Archie away from her best friend Betty at every turn! The three always find themselves in a crazy love triangle—one that has no end in sight! That being said, even when she's competing with Betty for a date with Archie, their friendship manages to stay intact. As the heiress to Lodge Industries, her bottomless wallet allows Veronica to be the ultimate fashionista. This leads to her having the hottest fashions in town! She wants the best money can buy… even if Archie's pockets are filled with lint!

Despite her expensive taste, Ronnie's heart is second only to the size of her mansion. Adjusting to small-town life wasn't easy for Veronica, but she's managed to forge some unbreakable bonds— especially with her best friend Betty.

DID YOU KNOW?

- Veronica is actually allergic to plastic. She actually maxes out all her credit cards so she won't have to hold onto them for too long!

- Veronica has approximately fifteen pet dogs, all white poodles named Fifi. This may sound confusing, but we assure you it's efficient.

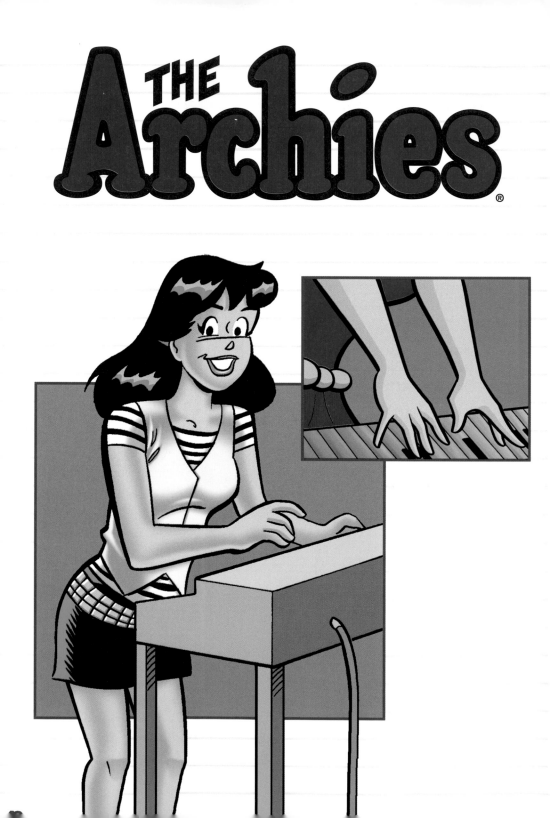

Veronica demonstrates her twinkle fingers on keyboards in The Archies, as well as provides additional backup vocals along with Betty. Veronica might not have the drive or passion behind lyric-writing as Archie and Betty do, but she's got the money and resources to make sure The Archies always headline gigs and go on tours without having to rough it. No broken-down vans and seedy motels for these musicians, nothing but luxury tour buses and five-star hotels!

Archie
FRESHMAN YEAR

Veronica spent her freshman year of high school even more cultured and learned than before, thanks to a holiday break spent travelling the globe! As such, it inspired a desire in her to explore her more dramatique side, namely working with the Riverdale High Dramatic Arts Players! Her newly discovered thespian side didn't, however, prevent her from getting real and arguing with Betty over Archie's affection!

In the hip '90s makeover of the Little Archies, Veronica resumed her place on the throne as queen of junior high! Sporting her signature big bow, pink sunglasses, and mismatched star earrings (style in the '90s was wild!), Veronica had no problem getting everyone to notice her. Despite that, she still often found herself competing for Archie's affection (what can we say? Ladies loved the mullet!) while Reggie did the same for her!

little Archie
and his pals

Veronica Lodge may not have made her big move to Riverdale until she was a teen, but Riverdale is in all of its citizens DNA, even if they weren't born there, and as such Veronica has somehow transcended space and time to have experiences with her Riverdale friends even as a child. Much as she does later In life, Little Veronica has no problem flaunting her wealth and possessions, always having the best and biggest birthday parties, and all the coolest and shiniest toys on the block!

WORLDS OF VERONICA

Veronica joined her BFF Betty as a super-agent on patrol in Riverdale! Wearing the sleekest and chic-est black leather spy outfit, "Agent V" works with Agent B to fight for truth, justice, and the Riverdale way! It's thanks to Veronica's father, Hiram Lodge, that the two have access to all sorts of technicological advancements in his hi-tech crimefighting facility (he and Dilton Doiley are also the only two people who knows the true identities of Riverdale's own Spy Girlz!)

While it may be thanks to her father's hi-tech facility and Dilton's fancy gadgetry that Agent B gets business done—but as a part of the Explorers of the Unknown, Veronica—better known as Angel Love—is the resident martial arts expert on the team! No foes stand a chance against her deadly karate chops and sweeping kicks!

Veronica was a certified scream queen in the world of *Archie's Weird Mysteries*. When not yelping in fright, she's funding the efforts of the Teen Scene Investigators. Also, at one point she became 50-ft tall, but that's whole different story...

It took a little longer before Veronica found her superpowers, but in 1996 she officially affiliated herself with the SuperTeens. With her sleek black and pink outfit and ability to scream extremely loudly (usually thanks to stress), she could shatter windows and knock people out.

It takes any good superhero sometime to fine-tune her powers, and the same was true for Veronica, who later switched from the vain Miss Lodge to a powerful teen—literally, she became PowerTeen, a comic character originally created by comic fan, artist, and fellow teen Chuck Clayton. As PowerTeen, Veronica uses her smarts and agility to outsmart even the most formidable villains!

Veronica's globe-trotting ways were never more clearly documented than in her own series, *Veronica's Passport*, which saw the well-traveled teen all over the world, in locations like Paris, New York, Rome, Mumbai, and more!

But Veronica's jet setting wasn't just about trying on the finest fashions and enjoying the beautiful scenery each city and country has to offer. Whether it was getting involved with an international jewel thief in Paris or attending business school in Rome, on her journeys Veronica also had quite a few unforgettable experiences and important lessons learned!

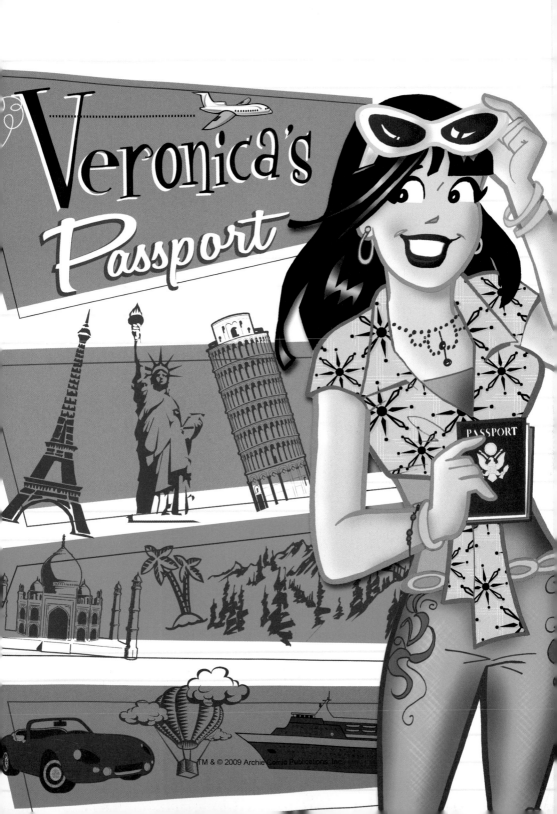

Veronica's *Passport*

AFTERLIFE with Archie

In the zombie-plagued *Afterlife with Archie* universe, Veronica lives alone with her father Hiram, as her mother Hermione passed when she was younger. The spacious mansion she shares with her father and dutiful butler Smithers becomes the gang's refuge at the beginning of the outbreak, until the zombies descend upon it, forcing an evacuation. Veronica tries her best to stay strong in the face of what's happening while also dealing with feelings of rejection thanks to the engagement of Archie and Betty. This also doesn't make things easier between Hiram and Archie, who do not share many of the same views concerning the outbreak.

VAMPIRONICA

…But that's not Veronica's only foray into the horror world. While she may be struggling to stay afloat in the zombie outbreak, she's patient zero in the vampire epidemic that arrived in Riverdale. In the miniseries *Vampironica*, Veronica discovers that her parents were attacked by a centuries-old vampire and turned into the immortal and bloodthirsty. Upon also being attacked, she soon turns a few others to the dark side. But thanks to help from Dilton Doiley, Veronica assembles a team to take down the malicious vampires and end the curse of the originator—or so she thought. Veronica's constantly in a battle between trying to be a normal teen while also hiding her bloodsucking ways.

Betty & Veronica Vixens

And speaking of having teeth— Veronica's got a lot of bite in *Vixens*, where she joins best friend Betty as the leader of their all-girl motorcycle gang. Tired of having to put up with the boys' silly acts of showboating, Veronica's not only looking for thrill, but to show she's more than just a rich debutante, she can hold her own, too. She does use her money, though, to buy the ladies the best bikes around. If she's going to lead a motorcycle gang, there's no doubt they're going to be riding in style!

RIVERDALE

Veronica, played by Camila Mendes, was originally born in Riverdale to parents Hiram and Hermione Lodge. Shortly after her birth, her family moved to New York City, where she lived a life of luxury and privilege, and she attended private schools, where she was a cheerleader and a bully. However, this all changed when her father was convicted of fraud and embezzlement. He was sent to jail, and Veronica and her mother were depleted of their fortune and subjected to malicious gossip. She and her mother left New York for Riverdale to start a new life, with Veronica determined to change her icy and hard-partying ways.

At Riverdale High, Veronica soon became a member of the cheerleading team the River Vixens. Upon her arrival in Riverdale, Veronica sought to reform herself into a better person and befriended Betty in the process. She was also in a relationship with Archie. The pair called it quits on a few occasions, but in the end always get back together. During their second breakup, she had a brief romance with Reggie while Archie dated Josie.

When Archie's father Fred was shot, Veronica looked at her parents as prime suspects, accusing them of hiring a hit man to kill Fred due to his refusal of selling his shares of the company upon Hermione's request. With the discovery of her parents' secret purchase of Pop's Chock'lit Shoppe, Veronica was able persuade them into granting her a more involved role in Lodge Industries. Not long after being accepted into her father's inner circle, Veronica would soon realize the truth behind his intentions for Riverdale and how he handled his business dealings. Determined to make up for her father's wrongdoings, Veronica attempted to stop his monopolizing of the Southside. She did this by purchasing the Whyte Wyrm bar and later using it to cut a deal with her father for the Chock'lit Shoppe in exchange. Hiram agreed to make the exchange, but as a result of this, he also stripped Veronica of all her duties to Lodge Industries, as well as cutting her off completely from using his money. This was but one of many deeper-rooted feuds between Veronica and her father. Veronica then became the proud owner of the Chock'lit shop as well as the founder of the La Bonne Nuit speakeasy until returning ownership to Pop Tate before leaving for college.

Betty and Veronica

How can two people who are polar opposites that fight over the same guy for over 80 years still manage to remain BFFs? The question has stumped friends, family, pop culture historians, educators, and psychologists alike for decades. And yet, Betty Cooper and Veronica Lodge continue to not only remain friends, but grow their friendship each and every year.

While Betty is the middle class, girl-next-door to Veronica's upper class, heiress-in-the-making, their varied lifestyles only serve to strengthen their overall bond. Over the years their friendship has evolved from two young women constantly undermining each other to win their red-headed love's affections, to two strong, independent, determined young women who lift each other up.

We've seen the trials and tribulations of high school friendship from freshmen year all the way to senior year. We've seen them maintain relationships as adults, even if one of them happened to be married to Archie. We've also seen them unite as super spies, gang leaders, even co-presidents! Betty and Veronica just work better together! If there's one thing that's for certain, Betty and Veronica have an unbreakable bond—and one that's proven to stand the tests of time. A friendship we should all be so lucky to have!

JUGHEAD JONES

First Appearance: *Pep Comics* #22, 1941

Hair: Black

Eyes: Black (when he decides to open them)

Hobbies: Eating, cooking, eating what he's just cooked, hanging out with friends (while eating)

Likes: Eating, his sheepdog Hot Dog, his little sister Jellybean, relaxing

Dislikes: Working harder (when you could be working smarter), mean and uptight people, limited servings

Archie's iconic best friend was born Forsythe Pendleton Jones III. That's a mouthful, even for him, so everyone calls him by his nickname: "Jughead." He's always had Archie's back as a best friend should. He is the calm in the storm of Archie's often-chaotic life. When he isn't eating (which is rare) he likes to take it easy. He doesn't start drama and is too cool and laid back to get entangled in any.

Where he draws the line is bullies. Whether it's Reggie's pranks or Veronica's conceits, he'll take action when he feels like any of his friends are being wronged. Whether it's a sharp and witty retort or a cunning plan, Jughead will take them down a peg and then let bygones be bygones.

Jughead's personal distaste for romantic relationships aside, his next closest friend is Betty Cooper. He enjoys her upbeat and positive attitude and is the first to support her when the going gets rough (if Archie doesn't beat him to it). Other good friends include Dilton, since Jughead rolls with the techno-babble, and Moose, who enjoys Jughead's low-key and easy-going company.

DID YOU KNOW?

-Jughead's signature "crown" is actually a stylized beanie called a "whoopie cap." It's traditionally made by cutting up the brim of a fedora, which is then folded upward. It was popular among kids and mechanics in the 1920s and 1930s. Somehow, Jughead has managed to keep it stylish for the better part of a century!

THE Archies

When you're somebody's best pal, sometimes you agree to play in the band that's named after them without question. Jughead plays the drums, usually avoiding the spotlight but supporting his friends with the tempo and beat. When he does provide vocals, Jughead has a surprisingly rich bass singing voice.

Jughead likes to keep things simple. Typically, his drum set consists of: a bass drum, a floor tom, a snare drum, and a ride cymbal. It may seem rudimentary compared to other bands' set-ups, but Mr. Jones knows how to get the most out of his hardware.

FRESHMAN YEAR

Jughead may seem like a stable fixture of Riverdale, but he actually spent his freshman year of high school in Silby, Montana! His carefree attitude and aloof nature made him the odd kid out at Silby High, but did catch the eye of a young girl named Sadie. She just about charmed Jughead out of his steadfast bachelor life, but circumstances brought Jughead back to Riverdale.

Jughead was the tallest and leanest of the crew with his decidedly crown-shaped hat balanced perfectly atop his luscious pompadour. Regardless of age or media, he retained his love for burgers and disdain for complications. He was often seen cruising through life with his headphones on. He was voiced by Michael Fantini in the animated version.

little Archie
and his pals

Some friendships last a lifetime. Jughead started his with Archie when they were wee elementary students. Even then Little Jughead's casual, laid-back nature had him as a voice of reason to temper Little Archie's wild imagination.

It was here Jughead first started his love for food and donning his signature whoopie hat. Too young to be in the kitchen, he constantly grazed on snacks—both his own, and whatever his friends left unattended.

WORLDS OF JUGHEAD

CAPTAIN HERO ™

When trouble arises, Jughead takes on the title of Captain Hero. In addition to flight and superhuman physicality, he has the super power to eat anything. We don't mean his usual iron stomach that can handle any meal, we mean anything—matter, energy, or otherwise! You might think his hat would be a liability to his secret identity, but it's really the source of his power! By donning his cap, he transforms with this incantation:

Teeny weenie magic beanie
Pointing towards the sky!
Bring me muscle, vigor, strength
Form a super guy!

Archie's EXPLORERS OF THE UNKNOWN! ™

Jughead, otherwise known to his fellow Explorers of the Unknown as "Squint Jones," ditched his usual laid-back style for life in the fast lane. Squint was the team's resident daredevil and escape artist!

Jughead is whisked away once again to save reality; this time via a magic stool that transports him to the dimension of Dinerville. The series, which ran from 1990-1991, pitted Jughead against the vile real estate agent Sal Monella to save the lives and livelihoods of Dinerville's uniquely quirky residents.

Jughead was the team's "foodologist." You'd think that's just a made-up term so he could snack on the job, but in reality Jughead's acute sense of smell and keen eye for food led to numerous insights and breakthroughs. (And "foodologist" is totally a thing. We looked it up. Trust us!)

Jughead's Time Police

Jughead doesn't like to think too hard, so you wouldn't suspect he'd be the hero of all space and time! In the original series (1990-1991), Jughead was recruited by the Time Police to correct errors throughout history. His partner was January McAndrews, Archie's distant descendant. In the 2019 reboot, it's Jughead who causes problems in the time-stream, prompting Officer McAndrews to action.

FORSYTHE P. JONES
DEPUTY MARSHAL

Sometimes in this crazy old world, you need a private investigator with iron will, keen eye, and fearless resolve. And when you can't find them, you settle for Jughead.

After binge watching the latest noir detective film, Jughead donned a trench coat and played around with acting like a stereotypical gumshoe. The problem was he looked the part too well, and his natural talents of observation made him a surprisingly adept detective.

With the promise of burgers, catered meals, and bottomless refills, Jughead answered the call for justice from numerous victims in and around Riverdale. He called upon his friends and their connections to check all the angles (and do most of the legwork so he wouldn't have to!)

The usually laid-back Jughead had to be quick on his feet as the criminals he was closing in on often lashed out in vicious ways. Whether it was cutting his car brakes or shoving him off scaffolding, Jughead nearly joined the big buffet line in the sky more than once.

In one case he was hired to find the thief of a secret, experimental device. What he uncovered was a family drama driven by lies and love. In another, a rising star was making her leap from television to cinema but appeared to be targeted by an unknown saboteur. Jughead discovered it wasn't out of malice, or even jealousy, but that she was a pawn in a larger grifting scheme.

As Jughead's reputation grew, so did the scope of his cases. He uncovered a conspiracy at the coastal amusement park. It had once been part of his fondest childhood memories but had become a front for a smuggling operation. He even uprooted a burglary ring by finding the unlikely shadowy ringleader: a charismatic club owner who was using his unwitting teen hires!

So, the next time you need a hardboiled flatfoot with ice in his veins, maybe settle for the guy who wants the hardboiled egg sandwich and an ice-cold malt instead. He gets results!

AFTERLIFE with Archie

It all began with the unthinkable: Jughead's beloved sheepdog Hot Dog was hit by a car. Desperate to save his pet, Jughead convinced Sabrina to break magical taboo and resurrect Hot Dog. What came back was not the dog he loved, but something darker. Jughead was bitten by the undead Hot Dog and slowly, painfully, succumbed to the zombie curse of his own making.

Jughead then became "Patient Zero" for a zombie outbreak that would devastate Riverdale, and later the world. While his rotting body led the zombie apocalypse, his spirit endured as his former self. Only Archie could see or hear him, but the freedom of (un)death allowed Jughead to share his previously reserved thoughts.

JUGHEAD
THE HUNGER

Jughead's insatiable appetite is legendary. What if we told you it's because he's from a long line of werewolves? Mild-mannered by day, wild and ravenous by night, Jughead is horrified to learn he's the serial murderer known as the "Riverdale Ripper!" Jughead's struggle with his curse costs him dearly and pits him against his childhood friends.

RIVERDALE

One constant in the universe is Jughead is always Archie's lifelong pal. Played by Cole Sprouse on The CW's *Riverdale*, Jughead is often the narrator of ongoing events. He is a gifted writer, first contributing to various high school newspapers, and then becoming a renowned book author. Jughead's pursuit of truth and justice—both in written word and deed—drives him to root out the darker elements in Riverdale and protect his friends.

SOUTH SIDE SERPENTS

Originally, the Southside Serpents were a rival group of kids who bullied Little Archie and his friends. In Riverdale, they were reimagined as an international criminal organization. The local chapter was led for a time by Jughead's father, F.P. Jones, and regularly gathered at the Whyte Wyrm bar. Jughead inherited the title of "Serpent King" and did his best to manage his new criminal empire before finding his own way out.

REGGIE MANTLE

First Appearance: *Jackpot Comics* #5, 1942

Hair: Greasy. We mean… black.

Eyes: Brown

Hobbies: Pranks (he is the self-styled King of April Fools' Day), schemes, tom-foolery, chicanery, practical jokes, and generally being a pain

Likes: Himself, money, attention, Midge, Archie's gullibility and friendship, his dachshund Vader

Dislikes: Rules, consequences, Archie's friendship (it's… complicated)

Reginald "Reggie" Mantle is all about one person: himself. He sees himself as the smartest, smoothest, and most stylish guy in Riverdale and he wants everyone to know it. When not scheming his way to the top of the social ladder, Reggie delights himself by playing pranks on others. It doesn't matter who you are or what you do, you're fair game in Reggie's eyes. While these pranks are usually harmless, the knowledge that Reggie may strike at any moment earns him few friends and even less sympathy. There's one thing everyone can count on, though: there's never a dull moment when Reggie's around!

His relationship with Archie is complicated. Archie's good and giving nature makes him an easy mark for Reggie's cunning. Archie's popularity also makes him a target of Reggie's lashing out due to his own insecurities. But for all the trouble he causes, Archie is still willing to forgive and forget—he'll always give Reggie one more chance. That makes him Reggie's one reliable friend, and Reggie really isn't quite sure how to handle that.

DID YOU KNOW?
-Reggie debuted on his own in 1942's *Jackpot Comics* #5 and went on to be folded into the greater Archie universe later. The most notable appearance was *Archie's Rival Reggie*, which began in 1949. Over time and a few name changes, the title became *Reggie and Me* in 1966 and ran all the way to 1980.

THE Archies

With all the problems he's caused, you wouldn't expect Reggie to be a welcomed member of the band. However, Reggie's desire to perform and excel keep him on track and allow him to be a valued member of the ensemble. Reggie plays bass, even filling in on lead guitar if Archie isn't available, and joins in on vocals.

Despite his commitment to the act, Reggie's ego is still a bit of a problem. He aims to outperform his bandmates, which doesn't always make for the best harmony. He's also gone so far as to hire his own fans to infiltrate the band's gigs and scream his name, making him seem more popular. In the television version of the band, featured on The CW's *Riverdale*, it's Kevin who plays bass instead of Reggie.

little Archie

and his pals

It's not fair to say "some kids are born rotten," but Little Reggie is the exception that proves the rule. While too young to pursue the more intricate pranks of his teenage self, Little Reggie is still a problem on the playground.

Whether it's simple pranks (like rubber snakes) or filching somebody's juice box, one has to keep an eye on the little weasel. While he's bothersome, he's not malicious—he's just doing what he thinks is funny. When one of the other children gets truly upset, Little Reggie feels guilty and will try—awkwardly—to make amends.

FRESHMAN YEAR

Reggie talks a big game, and he likes to pick on the freshmen, but he was on the receiving end himself in his own freshman year. He thought he'd hit it big by getting in close with the upper classmen but was really just their errand boy. It was a bitter pill to swallow and a rare moment of humility and self-reflection for him.

Reggie was as conceited and conniving as ever in this reimagining of the Riverdale kids. Though younger he was no less ego-driven and a poor sport. He was quick to find a reason for revenge and would go to great lengths to prank or undermine others to ensure they got what he thought they "deserved." Sometimes this tunnel vision made him miss the fact he was being used by Veronica to get her own revenge. He was voiced by Sunny Besen Thrasher in the cartoon version.

WORLDS OF REGGIE

EVILHEART™

Reggie is the antithesis to Archie in many ways, but not quite as pronounced as his alter-ego "Evilheart." Using the same PH Factor as Pureheart, Evilheart shares all the same powers but none of the weaknesses. If anything, his super-charged vices are hard to relinquish when the battles are through.

Can we get a time-out? Does he even count as a "superhero"? Sure, he helps take down the worse bad guys, but that seems like coincidence most of the time. What do we call him then? "Anti-hero"? "Anti-*villain*"?

Meanwhile, in the daydreams of Jughead, Reggie took the whole "evil superhero" thing to a new level. (Sidenote: seriously, isn't he technically a supervillain?!) As the head of Mantle Industries, Reggie created the violent robotic Ultrateens to replace the wholesome Superteens. When confronted over his schemes, he donned a suit of super-powered armor and the name "Iron Mantle."

(Yes, okay, he's working in the superhero business. But he's evil! Evil!)

Archie's EXPLORERS OF THE UNKNOWN!

Reggie's explosive personality made him suited for a very particular role in the Explorers of the Unknown. That's right, say hello to "Nitro Mantle"—explosives and demolitions expert!

Archie's WEIRD MYSTERIES

As a part of the Archie's Weird Mysteries crew, Reggie plays the role of the narcissistic, self-confident jock. So, not much has changed from regular Reggie's life! Unfortunately, his egotistical ways sometimes get the best of him, and make it hard for his pals to come up with good reasons to save him from the supernatural monsters that often overtake the town! No matter what, though, they always come through for their pal—for better or for worse!

RIVERDALE

Reggie has led numerous double lives in The CW's *Riverdale*. He was the darling captain of the high school football team, but was the culprit of a controversy at Riverdale High. Later in life he had a respected position in Hiram Lodge's employ and was coaching football, but both were fronts for illegal activities that endangered the students. It went a step further as he appeared a loyal lackey to Mr. Lodge, but was truly conspiring with Veronica to expose Hiram's criminal activity and bring him down.

His time with Veronica was just as much a roller-coaster ride as the rest of his life. Their passionate affairs burned bright and brief as Veronica was repeatedly drawn back to Archie. Reggie and Veronica's business ventures and rendezvous were frequent, impassioned, but always brief.

Reggie was played by Ross Butler in the first season, and then by Charles Melton thereafter.

KEVIN KELLER

First Appearance: *Veronica* #202, September 2010
Hair: Blonde
Eyes: Blue
Hobbies: Eating, journalism, archery, ROTC
Likes: Good food and hanging out with friends
Dislikes: Dishonesty, rudeness, bullies, healthy snacks like fruits (even if they're covered in chocolate!)

Kevin is a relatively new face in Riverdale. He had a lonely time as a kid, moving from place to place as his father was stationed at various military bases. He managed to find a lasting friendship with Wendy and William between moves, and found a vast and welcoming group of friends within Riverdale High.

Kevin is generally easy going and pleasant, lighting up the room when he enters. But beneath that casual demeanor is an iron core that allows him to stand up for his friends without hesitation.

DID YOU KNOW?
-Kevin has a huge appetite and a broad palette, but he's allergic to strawberries! …and by "allergic" we mean refuses to eat them. If there's one thing Kevin hates, it's dishonesty—and that includes fruit not being sweet!

LIFE WITH Archie®

Life with Archie took a look at two possible futures for Archie: one where he married Betty and one where he married Veronica. Both paths saw their friends and family grow and change in different ways, but there were a few constants throughout both.

One of those was the future for Kevin. He enlisted shortly after graduation and served multiple tours in the Middle East, rising to the rank of lieutenant. During one engagement he was wounded while rescuing a squad mate. The road to recovery was long and grueling, and his usual sunny disposition was clouded with anger and guilt.

Helping him through the struggles was Dr. Clay Walker. Kevin's bitterness started them off on the wrong foot, but time and reflection allowed them to meet again as friends. That friendship quickly blossomed into romance, and it wasn't long until the two were engaged.

The two were wed by the Mayor of Riverdale— Moose Mason in one instance, Winslow Glibb in the other—and were all set for their happily ever after.

It was interrupted when Clay was shot during a robbery. While he survived, Kevin was driven to make America safer for everyone. He ran for congress on a staunch gun control platform. This earned him as many enemies as it did supporters, and one disturbed person took it upon themselves to assassinate Kevin. Archie intervened, saving Kevin—but at the cost of his own life.

In the 10th Anniversary return to *Life with Archie*, Kevin's life had taken a different route. Now an EMT and practicing nurse at the local hospital, he was present when Hiram Lodge took a turn for the worse. In one scenario, he opted to join Archie as he reformed his band—even if it is was a crazy idea!

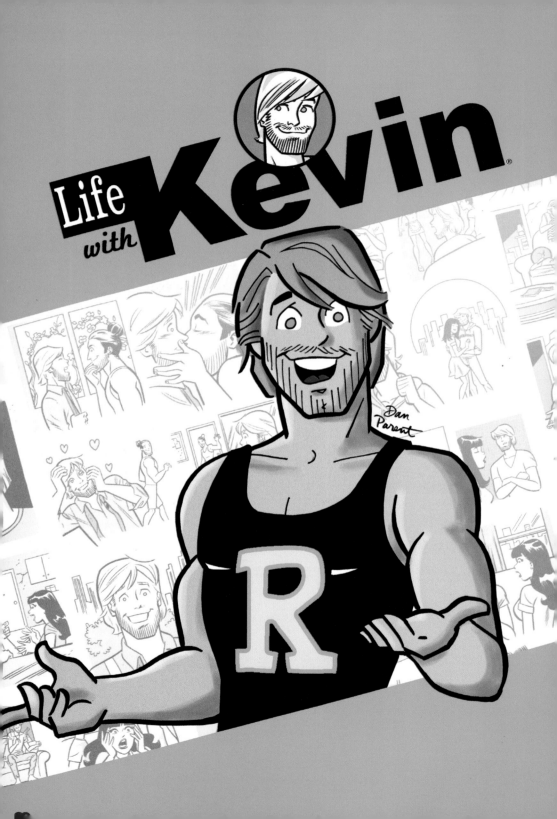

Life with Kevin was yet another possibility for Kevin's future. Instead of enlisting or getting his medical degree, Kevin majored in journalism and set out to stake his claim in New York City.

His apartment was lousy, his job at NYC-TV was tacky, and every other day he was ready to walk off the job. Things got even more hectic when Veronica arrived to crash at his place! She'd been kicked out of the house and cut off from the family fortune by her father. Not only could she not hold down a job to cover rent, but she kept inadvertently sabotaging Kevin's love life.

Kevin's charisma and rugged good looks netted him numerous opportunities—both for his career and romantic options—leaving him busy but ultimately directionless. It was only after his father had a medical scare that Kevin was able to focus, reevaluate, and set a new goal: teaching abroad!

RIVERDALE

Unlike his comic book counterpart, Kevin is a native to Riverdale and one of Betty's life-long friends. His mother serves in the Navy, rather than his father in the Army; however his father is the town's sheriff.

Kevin had a rocky love life in high school, struggling with issues of commitment and boundaries. Upon graduation he attended Carnegie Mellon with aspirations of breaking

into show business. Instead he ended up returning to Riverdale.

Once back home, he'd became a multi-disciplined teacher at Riverdale High and went on to win Teacher of the Year, although the honor served as a bitter reminder of the dreams he hadn't achieved. Kevin is played by Casey Cott.

CHERYL BLOSSOM

First Appearance: *Betty & Veronica #320, 1982*
Hair: Red
Eyes: Green
Hobbies: Attention, money, villainy
Likes: Herself, getting her way, calculated revenge, her twin brother Jason is ok
Dislikes: Facts, being denied anything, other people's happiness, incriminating evidence

Cheryl Blossom is the extreme version of Veronica. Where Veronica holds everything to a (sometimes impossibly) high standard due to her wealth, Cheryl flaunts her own financial status and lords over her "lessers." Where Veronica can be a bit selfish at times, Cheryl is unapologetically all-consuming. Where Veronica might pull some strings to get her way, Cheryl willfully and gleefully sets out to cause drama and chaos.

Cheryl and her family originally lived in the upscale region of Pembrooke. Due to financial concerns, the Blossoms moved to Riverdale. Despite her disdain for her "less sophisticated" peers, Cheryl couldn't help but be tempered by the charm and sincerity of Riverdale High. She had to walk a fine line between keeping up appearances with her old classmates at Pembrooke High and being accepted in her new neighborhood—as the reigning queen bee of popularity, of course.

Cheryl is yet another girl who has fallen for Archie's charms. While the attraction is sincere, she gets just as much delight stoking the jealousy of Betty and Veronica, just to get a reaction.

DID YOU KNOW?
-Despite her often-selfish behavior, Cheryl is actually quite kind to animals. In addition to doting on her Pomeranian, Sugar, she spends some of her free time helping out at animal shelters.

Cheryl Blossom QUEEN B

One of Cheryl's hallmark adventures was when she defended her kingdom from foreign powers. No, this isn't one of those crazy spin-off adventures— this was the real deal!

Cheryl was the self-appointed "queen" of Pembrooke Academy. Her fortune and popularity had won her position as class president and a whole "hive" of minions answering her every beck and call.

The status quo was shaken to its core with the arrival of Pieter. He and his very wealthy family had immigrated from Norway and he was turning heads.

Kind, sociable, and dashingly handsome, Pieter was quick to make friends with everyone at the school. It didn't matter what their social standing was, or what clique they belonged to, Pieter was sociable with all of them. When Cheryl tried to gently (we said "gently," not "tactfully") have Pieter observe her hierarchy, he simply told her "no." Such shock! Such scandal!

But there was more to Pieter than it seemed. His parents wanted greater clout in the school community so they could receive more donations for their conservation work. They pushed Pieter to assimilate as quickly as possible to snatch up the class presidency and even went so far as to conspire with the headmaster to rig the election!

Cheryl was forced to take drastic measures. She recruited Veronica to help her scheme. She willingly talked to people outside her social circle. She allowed herself to see herself among "commoners." And the most drastic action of all: she worked hard to win the election legitimately!

The effort paid off as the student body demanded a recount, exposing the election fraud. Pieter, ashamed of his own manipulations, offered to make peace. In the end, Cheryl got what she wanted: her throne, her adoring subjects, and a date with Pieter. All hail the queen!

AFTERLIFE with Archie

Times of crisis can bring out the best in people—and the worst. As the world descended into chaos, Jason let the worst of himself take over. One fateful day, Cheryl and Jason went off into the woods together. Only Cheryl came back, rechristening herself as "Blaze."

Betty & Veronica Vixens

Betty and Veronica built their own biker gang from the ground up to protect Riverdale. Cheryl realized what they were up to and invited herself into the gang—to a lukewarm response. Her aggressive attitude and attempts to become gang leader started causing friction almost immediately. But ultimately Cheryl's intentions were good, and she became a key member of the gang, unified with the girls to stop the evils threatening the women of their town.

BLOSSOMS 666

Cheryl and her twin brother Jason are the most popular students at Riverdale High. They're wealthy, fashionable, and everyone wants to be them. Their family also happen to be Satanists, and between Cheryl and her brother, one of them is the Anti-Christ.

Of course, deciding who gets to be the most evil goes beyond normal sibling rivalry (who would've guessed!). The siblings compete to see what sinister misdeeds they can force their friends and classmates to engage in, to increasingly frightening results. Ever observant Betty Cooper catches onto their schemes, and is determined to stop their reign of evil over Riverdale. She does so by befriending a fellow student who's also taken notice, Julian. Betty learns that Julian is actually Cheryl and Jason's long-lost triplet brother, but what she doesn't realize is that he is also in the running for the title of Anti-Christ. Cheryl and Jason realize that they'll need to come together if they're going to win this, and their main priority becomes ending Julian.

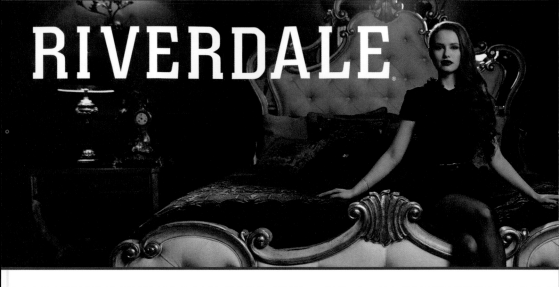

RIVERDALE

Portrayed by Madeline Petsch in The CW's *Riverdale*, Cheryl seems to be cursed. Her brother Jason was clearly favored over her, and his death made her a pariah in her own home. Her attempts to reign as the "queen bee" at Riverdale High were a cover for someone deeply troubled and alone. Her relationship with Toni Topaz saw them through a myriad of trials including a brief stint within the Southside Serpents and their own attempts to rival them as the Pretty Poisons, although that venture eventually failed.

When Jason's body was exhumed, Cheryl confiscated it and tried to keep it. She treated Jason as if he were still alive and there to confide in.

Eventually Toni and Penelope were able to get through to her, have her end the macabre spectacle, and finally put Jason to rest.

But things didn't magically turn around for Cheryl—if anything, they only got darker from there. Toni's nana believed Cheryl's family to be a plague on Riverdale, which prompted Cheryl to redeem the Blossom family's honor, turning away from her girlfriend Toni and her college education.

Believing that she would be doomed to live a life of unhappiness, Cheryl lived in isolation in the rebuilt Thornhill mansion. She also discovered that her ancestor Abigail Blossom was a witch burned at the stake many years ago. When no one in Riverdale would apologize for how her ancestor was treated, she invoked Abigail's curse—leading her to be possessed by Abigail. Once again, her friends freed her from this possession—though Cheryl did emerge from it with pyrokinetic abilities.

TONI TOPAZ

First Appearance: *Jughead Double Digest* #176, December 2011

Hair: Pink (the curls are natural, the color we're pretty sure is a dye job)

Eyes: Brown

Hobbies: Competitive eating
Likes: Friendly competition, earnestness, cupcakes

Dislikes: Dishonesty, loudmouths, show-offs

Some call her "Two-Fisted Toni." Some call her just plain "Toni." But she'd really prefer you not call her by her full name, Antoinette Topaz. (We think it sounds just fine, but it's her choice.) Toni is self-assured and lives life with a confident swagger. While she has the same misgivings as any teenager, Toni faces them with ferocious confidence and is always happy to lend that energy to her friends.

While Toni can be found hanging out with the familiar Riverdale gang, she primarily runs in a crew of three with her BFFs Snarky and Hammer. They may sound abrasive, but remember, this is "Two-Fisted Toni" we're talking about. You're in good hands with them. (Not necessarily gentle hands, but still…)

DID YOU KNOW?

- Toni holds the rare title of someone who defeated Jughead in an eating contest. There were extenuating circumstances, so Toni longs for the day she can compete against him fair and square.

RIVERDALE.

Toni of The CW's *Riverdale* has led a much wilder, more dangerous life than her comic counterpart. On the surface she was just Jughead's friend after he transferred to Southside High. Together they revitalized the school paper, *The Red and Black*, where she acted as their photographer.

Her sinister secret was that she was a low-level member of the Southside Serpents, which was run by Jughead's father at the time. She helped initiate him into the gang. After transferring to Riverdale High, she was quick to convert her new beau—Cheryl—into their ranks as well. Ironically, Jughead exiled her from the gang after he took control.

Toni and Cheryl, bitter over their exile, attempted to form a new gang: the Pretty Poisons. The venture was short-lived. As the new gang fell apart, so too did the girls' romance, although their friendship endured.

Seven years down the road, Toni had rebounded. She was a mother now, with her little Anthony enjoying two father figures: Fangs and Kevin. But Toni hadn't settled for a simple domestic life. She had not only rejoined the Southside Serpents, but ascended to the rank of Serpent Queen.

She's portrayed by Vanessa Morgan.

SOUTH SIDE SERPENTS

In the Riverdale-verse, Toni proudly leads the Southside Serpents biker gang as their Serpent Queen. She rose up in the ranks over the years, proving that she's both tough and committed to the gang that took her in ever since she was a wayward young teenager. Despite her confidence, she definitely felt some competition when FP Jones insisted on bringing his son, Jughead, into the fold. Not one to be de-throned due to nepotism, Toni made sure to keep an eye on Jughead, both as his competition and his protector.

JASON BLOSSOM

First Appearance: *Jughead #325*, October 1982

Hair: Red (and slightly darker than Cheryl's)

Eyes: Green (we're pretty sure those aren't colored contact lenses!)

Hobbies: Being rich, telling other people how much richer he is than them

Likes: Money, acknowledgement, being a twin (seriously, he makes it weird sometimes), Betty

Dislikes: Failure, losing, any degree of discomfort (physical or emotional)

PAT!
PAT!

Jason is Cheryl's twin brother—a fact he seems oddly proud of. This doesn't translate to peace between the siblings as Jason will be the first to mock Cheryl for her foibles or criticize one of her ideas. That said, if anyone else were to do so, he'd be the first to her defense.

Jason is quite proud of his status as one of the wealthy elites in Pembrooke and delights in lording his money and status over the "Townies" of Riverdale. That said, he can't help but be smitten with the down-to-earth Betty. He also holds a begrudging respect for Archie despite himself.

He holds everyone to an impossible standard, even those he counts as "friends," stepping over them if they fall.

DID YOU KNOW?
-He and Cheryl are twins! Wild, right? Bet you never saw that coming!

AFTERLIFE with Archie

Jason's fixation on his twin status is played for laughs normally, but it takes a far more sinister turn in this dark alternative take on things. Jason's obsession with Cheryl crossed the line into possessive amorousness, even as the world fell to the zombie apocalypse. The two of them went off into the wilds together, and only Cheryl returned. Jason was next seen as part of the undead, but we doubt it was a simple zombie bite that turned him.

BLOSSOMS 666

Jason and Cheryl competed for a dark honor against their long-lost third sibling, Julian. During the vile escapades, Jason was an adept manipulator, preying upon Jughead and Ethel. Ultimately Jason opts to ally with Cheryl to stop their estranged brother rather than allow him to win the competition.

RIVERDALE

Jason did not spend much time alive on The CW's *Riverdale*, but he still had a lasting impact. Everything began with his disappearance and death which shook the town to its core.

Jason first started dating Polly Cooper—Betty's older sister—as a way to gain clout amongst the other jocks at Riverdale; their relationship was a status symbol. In time, however, his feelings for her became real. Their passion led to the birth of twins Juniper and Dagwood.

Their relationship wasn't accepted by everyone. Betty saw through Jason's facade initially and maintained vigilance for the sake of her sister. Clifford Blossom, his father, didn't approve of him being with someone outside of their social circle.

Jason was being groomed to take control of the family's maple business. This made him the favored of the twins, but it didn't earn him any love. When Jason learned his father used the company as a front for a drug smuggling operation, he conspired to elope with Polly and disappear. Once Clifford found out, he shot and murdered his own son.

He's played by Trevor Stines.

DILTON DOILEY

First Appearance: *Pep Comics #78*, March 1950

Hair: Black

Eyes: Brown

Hobbies: SCIENCE! Which one? All of them.

Likes: Learning, studying, applying said learned study, athletics

Dislikes: Bullies, confrontation, pseudo-science, String Theory (extra dimensions? seriously?)

SOLAR HEATING SYSTEM

Dilton is the resident brainiac and universal homework/project helper for the students of Riverdale. Dilton happily shares his expertise with everyone, encourages everyone's studies, and usually explains things in terms they can understand. Sometimes. Okay, he occasionally gets too in the weeds, but he's still helpful!

Dilton's best friend is Moose. Despite the gap in cognitive abilities, the two are amazing in sync. Dilton helps Moose with his studies, and Moose protects Dilton from any would-be bullies. Dilton is also close to Chuck, who is the only one of his friends to know the secret that Dilton's father is actually his step-father.

In addition to regular academics, Dilton is always crafting inventions, gizmos, and whatchamacallits to help out the Riverdale gang. They usually work. Sometimes. Okay, they occasionally go haywire, but mistakes are part of progress!

DID YOU KNOW?

-Dilton aspires to be on the Riverdale High sports teams, but unfortunately doesn't have the physique to compete. To show his team spirit he dons the school's mascot costume!

Dilton received his own brief stint at stardom with his personal mini-series *Dilton's Strange Science*. He was joined by Danni Malloy, an aspiring inventor and a rare match for his intellect. Together they dealt with all sorts of—you guessed it—strange science. Dilton also grappled with his own love life, taking advice from Archie and Reggie. (C'mon, Dilly. We thought you were the smart one.)

Dilton and Danni's adventures revolved around testing out new inventions and dealing with the far-reaching consequences. In one case, Dilton showcased a shrink-ray of his own design. He and Danni were shrunk to the size of bugs and had to deal with the now gargantuan terrors of the backyard.

Even after they returned to normal size, the ray gun's potency caught the attention of aliens from the planet Zog. The invaders stole the shrink ray, prompting a high-speed, low-altitude chase over Riverdale.

In addition to (mis)adventures in science, Dilton offered the ready historical insight into everyday conveniences we take for granted. He also offered up simple experiments for readers to try at home.

AFTERLIFE with Archie

At the end of the world, you want the smartest person in the room with you. Lucky for Archie, Dilton was around. In addition to his vast practical knowledge, Dilton was a walking encyclopedia of horror movie tropes. In the middle of a zombie apocalypse, we guess that counts as "practical knowledge" too.

THUNK

VAMPIRONICA

When you suddenly find yourself to be a blood-sucking vampire, you want the smartest person in the room with you. Lucky for Veronica, Dilton was around. (We're sensing a trend here…) Dilton was Veronica's first ally in the fight to keep Riverdale free of the forces of evil.

JUGHEAD THE HUNGER

When you find yourself converted into a ravenous werewolf, you want to devour the smartest person in the room. Wait… what?! Run, Dilton! Whoops, too late. To make matters worse, his mad scientist of a cousin, Milton, resurrected Dilton as a zombie minion. Oh well—two out of three ain't bad, eh, Dilton?

RIVERDALE

Dilton was played by Major Curda for four seasons of The CW's *Riverdale*. Unlike his introverted comic counterpart, Dilton was an accomplished boy scout and a survivalist. This, unfortunately, stemmed from his father's over-reaction to the passing of Dilton's uncle. Darryl Doiley obsessively drilled his young son in all manners of extreme survivalist skills.

His "unique" upbringing sparked a love for firearms and probably played a part in him becoming an avid fan of conspiracy theories.

When the violent vigilante Black Hood began terrorizing Riverdale, Dilton was one of the few to join Archie's "Red Circle." Their goal was to bring Black Hood to justice, but ultimately became embroiled in a feud with the Southside Serpents. As the group faced its trials, Dilton was the only one to stay by Archie's side through it all, and suffered a stabbing for his efforts.

Later, Dilton came across the cursed game Gryphons & Gargoyles. Initially he thought it was a simple tabletop role-playing game, but soon uncovered its more sinister secrets. He tried to alert Jughead to its dangers, and that the villainous Gargoyle King was real, but he wasn't heeded. The next time anyone saw Dilton, he was the victim of a grizzly sacrificial rite.

MOOSE MASON

First Appearance: *Archie's Pal Jughead* #1, January 1949

Hair: Blonde

Eyes: Blue

Hobbies: Sports, looking after those in need

Likes: His girlfriend Midge, small children, animals, small words

Dislikes: Bullies, big words, anyone remotely within proximity to Midge

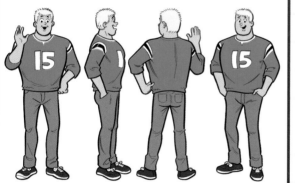

Marmaduke "Moose" Mason is a walking tank of a boy. He's normally a gentle giant, often unaware of his tremendous strength. Does it give him pause that he can bench-press a car? Nope. That's just how Moose is, and thank heavens he uses that power for good.

Moose is very protective at heart and will readily use his immense size and strength to stop bullies in their tracks and help those in need. It isn't elegant, but it's simple and direct—just the way Moose likes it.

However, that desire to protect sometimes crosses a line with his girlfriend, Midge. They're perfectly happy together, but if anyone so much as gives her a passing look, Moose flies into an overprotective fury. It's the one sticking point in the relationship, and Midge has gotten Moose to start thinking before acting.

DID YOU KNOW?
-It was later discovered that Moose had been dealing with long undiagnosed dyslexia. The Riverdale gang always helped him in his studies, but when the problem was identified, Moose was able to get the resources he needed to catch up.

Moose and Midge were at the school dance the night the zombie outbreak began. While they escaped with the others to Veronica's manor, Midge received a wound of dubious origin. Moose was concerned, but ultimately put his faith in Midge that she'd be fine. Unfortunately, that devotion left him vulnerable, and he was attacked the moment Midge turned. Their rampage in the manor was cut short when they were trapped under the pool's weather guard.

JUGHEAD THE HUNGER

It's hard to put down a moose. Mr. Mason's grim fate began with him hunting down Jughead to avenge Dilton. He was converted to a werewolf by Reggie, turning the normally intimidating young man into something truly frightening. His quest for revenge was cut short when he was killed by Elena's werewolf hunters.

He would not rest in peace, though, as his corpse was retrieved by Dilton's mad scientist of a cousin, Milton. The undead Moose was turned into a zombie slave, and then upgraded into the nightmarish "FrankenMoose" to once again do battle with Werewolf Jughead.

At that point, all he needed was to be a mummy and a vampire, and Moose will have completed his monster bingo card!

CHUCK CLAYTON

First Appearance: *Life with Archie* #110, June 1971

Hair: Black

Eyes: Brown

Hobbies: Comics - reading, drawing, studying, collecting (he'd love this book you're reading right now)

Likes: Football, hanging out, his girlfriend Nancy, drawing comics, researching his heritage

Dislikes: Germs, losing, being interrupted from drawing comics, and do not even get him started on the people who say "comics aren't art" because he'll tell you…!

Charles "Chuck" Clayton came to Riverdale when his father, Harry, took on a coaching position at Riverdale High. Chuck shared his father's athleticism and was a natural pick for the football and basketball teams, but his real passion is in comics. While an avid fan of the arts in general, Chuck is drawn to the magic of visual storytelling and aspires to be a professional comic book artist one day.

Chuck has an eye for the craft with clear and emotive designs that go beyond just being "a good drawing" and go on to convey whole characters and narratives. It's a passion that borderlines on obsession, and his longtime girlfriend Nancy sometimes has to drag him away from the drawing table to do things like, y'know, eat and touch grass.

DID YOU KNOW?
-Chuck's artistic prowess once won him prize money. He was pit against Veronica's high-profile professional artists and still pulled off the win. What did he do with the prize money? Supported his local comic shop, of course!

MIDGE KLUMP

First Appearance: *Pep Comics #257, 1971*
Hair: Black
Eyes: Blue
Hobbies: Cheerleading, studying psychology, astrology
Likes: Staying active, softball, shopping, platform shoes, reality TV, Reggie Mant— wait, no, that one's a mistake.
Dislikes: Possessiveness, people who litter, Reggie Mantle—maybe.

A lovely young lady and longtime friend of Betty & Veronica, Midge Klump has a history of being both beautiful and deadly. Midge's kindness makes her approachable, but any boys that come near should prepare for pain! Her boyfriend Moose tends to hide around waiting for a guy to chat her up. His intense jealousy has led to many beatings for friends and complete strangers alike! Reggie is known for his attempts at stealing Midge away—and the black eyes he receives soon after! Midge can sometimes grow upset with Big Moose over his temper and her mean-streak can emerge when another girl flirts with Moose as well. Although they seem like polar opposites, the pair remain deeply devoted to each other.

NANCY WOODS

First Appearance: *Pep Comics #309,*
January 1976

Hair: Black

Eyes: Brown

Hobbies: Shopping, girls' nights out, art,
writing

Likes: Fashion, art, writing, physical activities,
her boyfriend Chuck

Dislikes: Budgets, conflicting schedules, deadlines, Chuck's
tunnel vision. No, seriously, they had a date planned but he's
still drawing and…

Nancy Woods is a mainstay of Riverdale and one of Betty and Veronica's close friends. They all perform together in the Riverdale High cheerleading squad, and she's one of the premier players on the tennis and softball teams. When she's not showing off her athleticism, she can be found shopping for the latest styles with a keen eye for fashionable arrangements.

That attention to color, style, and form plays into her love of watercolor painting, and it's that shared love of the arts that she and Chuck bonded over. While she enjoys her art, she's sometimes frustrated that Chuck can't pry himself from his. On the other hand, she's demanded so much of his time he's missed his own sports commitments. The girl needs to find a balance!

DID YOU KNOW?
-Nancy is a lead writer and editor for the school newspaper *Blue & Gold*. How does she find time to fit all that into her day? No idea. Nancy! Teach us your ways!

ETHEL MUGGS

First Appearance: *Archie's Pal Jughead #84*, May 1962

Hair: Black

Eyes: Brown

Hobbies: Cooking and fine crafts

Likes: Sci-fi books, trains, art, trying new recipes, romantic thoughts, Jughead

Dislikes: Loneliness, judgemental people, meanness, lack of ingredients

"Big" Ethel Muggs stands apart from the crowd. In a town seemingly overpopulated with traditionally pretty girls, she doesn't look the part. And while Betty, Veronica, and her other friends love her for all her great qualities, Ethel has had to bear the brunt of awful name-calling. It's thanks to that close group of friends she's been able to learn to love herself for who she is.

Ethel has been called "boy-crazy" in the past, but it's more that she's in love with the concept of "love." And who wouldn't be? A partner through thick and thin, a friend and confidant, a romantic better half—we can see the appeal! For some reason she thinks she can find all that in Jughead, though, and he's not interested in any relationships.

What he is interested in is her cooking. Ethel is a wiz in the kitchen, crafting up meals and sweets that Jughead simply cannot resist. Their time together might be under a false pretense, but if they both acknowledge it, it's okay… right?

In Archie Comics' first ever webseries by Webtoon, Ethel is all grown up and ready to prove to the world that she's not the same shy, awkward teen she once was. She's a journalist in Brooklyn, New York, and living her best life—minus the whole never having a serious relationship, possibly getting evicted from her small apartment she shares with her roommate thing. She gets a call about a job that takes her back to her hometown of Riverdale. She takes the job with both excitement and trepidation—what will her friends (and foes) back in Riverdale think of her now? And what if they've all changed, too?

STACY BANKS

First Appearance: *Betty and Veronica Friends Forever: Summer Surf Party* #1, 2022

Hair: Dark Brown

Eyes: Brown

Hobbies: Creating mobile games and apps, participating in track and field, volleyball

Likes: Video games, coding, puzzles

Dislikes: Gossip, drama, hangers-on

Another of Riverdale's newest residents, Stacy Banks has set her sights on the world of STEM.

Her parents, George and Marsha Banks, are notable in the tech industry and work with Hiram Lodge, which means Veronica's looking to get in good with another member of the Riverdale elite. However, Stacy doesn't want to use their name alone to glide by.

She's an incredibly skilled coder who's made her own mobile games, and hopes to start her own video game company someday! She's down to earth, grounded, and looking to make genuine friendships with the teens in Riverdale.

DID YOU KNOW?
-Stacy may take coding—especially for video games—seriously. But her ultimate favorite arcade game? Pinball!

ELIZA HAN

First Appearance: *Archie & Friends: Summer Lovin'* #1, 2022

Hair: Black…or whatever color fits her mood.

Eyes: Brown

Hobbies: Puzzles, YA romance novels, DJing

Likes: Dating, hanging out with friends, and watching anime with her brother Darren

Dislikes: Bullies, know-it-alls, liars, ableists, people who use her

Last year, Eliza Han created a viral social media app that took the world by storm; she made a lot of money from it, but found out her "friends" were using her for clout. The Hans relocated to Riverdale to give their children a fresh new start and change of scenery.

Eliza is Black and Korean American, she's extremely proud of both of her heritages, her family, and being pansexual. She's free-spirited, a quick thinker, sarcastic, book and street smart, plus the owner of a huge heart that usually gets her in trouble. Eliza and her younger brother Darren are disabled—she has ADHD, thyroid disease, and type 1 diabetes, while her brother/best friend has Down's Syndrome.

DID YOU KNOW?

-Did you know that Eliza is a multi-millionaire business woman? Probably not, as she tends to keep her accomplishments a secret. When she's not working on her next business venture, Eliza can be found reading the latest YA romance novel, playing puzzles, DJing at parties, but most likely, she's watching anime with Darren.

GINGER LOPEZ

First Appearance: *Betty & Veronica Spectacular* #50, November 2001

Ginger is a more recent addition to the Riverdale crew, having moved from New York. She has rich tastes which she satisfies with her rich bank account. When not in class, she edits a teen-focused magazine and studies to become a professional fashion designer.

DID·YOU·KNOW?

-At one point, Ginger was being set-up to replace Cheryl in the Archie Universe. When Cheryl made her triumphant return, Ginger was spun off into her own (much nicer) character.

BRIGITTE REILLY

First Appearance: *Betty & Veronica Spectacular* #27, January 1998

Brigitte was an exchange student who enrolled in Riverdale High with trepidation. She soon found her place thanks to the friendliness of the Riverdale gang and her fantastic singing voice. She often partners up with fellow student Frankie Valdez to make beautiful music together, and rumor is she and Dilton have a bit of a thing going on!

DID·YOU·KNOW?

-Brigitte is such an impressive singer; she already has a deal with a major recording label!

HARPER LODGE

First Appearance:
Archie #656, August 2014

Harper is Veronica's cousin who normally lives across the country. When she visits, her vivaciousness turns heads. She and Ronnie typically get along— until her dear cousin starts snooping into Harper's love life! Harper is a children's author, has her own an advice column, and is an accomplished fashion designer. Even her wheelchair is customized by her!

DID·YOU·KNOW?

-Harper was injured in a car accident when she was little. Through multiple surgeries and years of physical therapy she's regained some limited mobility. Not that it ever slowed her down!

MARCY MCDERMOTT

First Appearance: *Veronica #137*, May 2003

Marcy is another of Veronica's cousins. Unlike Ronnie or Harper, she eschews high fashion and instead embraces the unconventional. She's a fan of science-fiction and all things nerdy which is entirely at odds with Veronica's whole vibe. Despite their differences, Marcy is eager and happy to help Veronica do whatever she needs.

DID·YOU·KNOW?

-Marcy's mother is Veronica's Aunt Elise. Aunt Elise remarried to wealthy widower Max Wells. The problem? Veronica had her eye on Max's son, Bryan. Except now they were all cousins. Whoops!

TRULA TWYST

First Appearance:
Archie's Pal Jughead #89, February 1997

Trula was a new student to Riverdale High and brought with her a passion for behavioral science. Her first target was the usually inscrutable Jughead. She managed to unravel the enigma that is Mr. Jones and went on to play him like a fiddle, earning her the awe and respect of the student body and a love-hate rivalry with Jughead himself.

DID·YOU·KNOW?

-Trula's control over Jughead's habits was so complete at one point she got him to give up junk food. Jughead! Giving up junk food! Can you imagine?

CRICKET O'DELL

First Appearance:
Archie #133, December 1962

Cricket has a unique talent: she can smell money and its value. Her sense of smell is so keen she can identify real treasures from counterfeits. She does have her limits, however, as extreme wealth can overwhelm her and knock her out. Otherwise, she's just another teen living life to her fullest in Riverdale. Y'know, a perfectly normal, money-sniffing girl.

DID·YOU·KNOW?

-Hiram Lodge has the same special ability as Cricket, and is notably disappointed that Veronica didn't inherit the skill. Could Cricket be yet another long-lost Lodge cousin?!

FRANKIE VALDEZ

First Appearance:
Archie #265, September 1977

Frankie can do it all: he can sing, he can dance, and he can play guitar. He's got talent for miles, and he knows it, leading to a bit of a swagger. He even managed to out-perform both The Archies and Brigitte! His relationship with Maria is passionate—with the highest of highs and the occasional explosive lows.

DID·YOU·KNOW?
-Given his look and his attitude, many have mistaken Frankie for Reggie. The confusion has led to a bit of a rivalry between the two.

MARIA RODRIGUEZ

First Appearance: *Archie's Girls Betty & Veronica #257*, May 1977

Maria came to Riverdale High when her father accepted the vice-principal position at the school. She was quick to fall for the handsome and talented Frankie and became his manager. Maintaining a romance is hard enough, but adding business into the mix makes for a volatile combination!

DID·YOU·KNOW?
-Maria's father essentially vanished after his initial appearance! What's the deal, Mr. Weatherbee?

RAJ PATEL

First Appearance: *Tales From Riverdale Digest* #21, August 2007

Raj is a relatively new student to Riverdale High, and with him he brings a passion for filmmaking. He always has his camcorder in hand and looking for the next great shot. While the students are impressed with his abilities, they can get tired of the lack of personal space. Raj also prides himself on his zero-budget special effects and hand-made props and models.

DID·YOU·KNOW?

-Raj's father, Dr. Patel, tolerates Raj's love of cinematography but wishes he'd take on more "serious" pursuits. To that we say: follow your dreams, Raj! You'll show him one day!

TINA PATEL

First Appearance: *Tales From Riverdale Digest* #21, August 2007

Tina is Raj's younger sister gifted with an incredible intellect. She takes after their father with a studious and serious nature. That's why Raj's flights of fancy and occasional scatter-brained antics drive her up the wall. He can turn her calm, cool demeanor into full blown rage in an instant and capture it all on film!

DID·YOU·KNOW?

-Tina should be a year behind Raj, but because of her academic success she skipped a grade and now studies alongside him!

KUMI TAMURA

First Appearance:
Betty and Veronica Digest #190, 2009

Kumi Tamura moved to the United States with her family from Japan. Upon arriving in Riverdale, she was amazed by how different it was from her homeland—from all of the American snacks at the supermarket to having her own bedroom at home! Kumi struggled at first with the English language, and her first day at Riverdale High was intimidating to say the least. But the kindness of her peers, namely Archie, Betty, Veronica, and Jughead, helped her to acclimate herself to her new setting with ease.

DID·YOU·KNOW?

-At home, Kumi's parents still maintain traditional Japanese customs and eat traditional Japanese meals and snacks— which is a dream for culinary-minded guests like Jughead!

TOMOKO YOSHIDA

First Appearance: *Betty* #108, March 2002

Tomoko Yoshida is a fellow student at Riverdale High and a member of the Green Girls. In addition to her volunteer efforts, she is also an excellent writer and works on Riverdale High's school paper, *The Blue and Gold*. Like Betty, her dream is to be a professional writer, though she also enjoys dabbling in art as well. While she may not yet up to be Chuck Clayton's skills, she improves with every stroke of her pen, often doodling and creating characters like the ones in her favorite manga series. Tomoko has a brother named Akira. We've also been introduced to a number of her relatives, including the Morizawas: her Aunt Grace, Uncle Roy, and their two young sons Shigeki and Royce.

DID·YOU·KNOW?

-To date, Tomoko has no steady boyfriend, although she occasionally attracts the attention of boys—fortunately, she's not looking to compete with anyone else for Archie's affection!

WENDY WEATHERBEE

First Appearance: *Tales From Riverdale Digest* #10, May 2006

The quirky and independent "Double W" was a big hit when she first came to Riverdale High. All the interest and popularity evaporated, however, when it came that out she was the niece of Principal Weatherbee. It's not that nobody trusts her, it's that they fear unwanted extra attention from her uncle!

DID YOU KNOW?

-In a school known for being a hotbed of relationship networking, Wendy is free of romantic advances everyone is too afraid of her uncle! It's a fact of life she's not too keen on.

BELLA BEAZLY

First Appearance:
Archie & Friends #136, December 2009

Nobody knew that lunch lady Ms. Beazly was married, let alone had a daughter! Bella filled in for her mother for a week at Riverdale High and caused quite the stir.

Her stunning good looks brought extra attendance to the cafeteria, but her stunningly poor skills in the kitchen left a bad taste in everyone's mouth.

DID YOU KNOW?

-Bella managed to fail upwards in a spectacular fashion. Veronica pulled some strings and got Bella her own cooking show—all to get her out of Archie's line of sight!

ADAM CHISHOLM

First Appearance: *Betty* #87 (July, 2000)

Adam Chisholm is a tall (taller than Archie!), lanky guy with a laid-back style. When he moved to Riverdale he immediately started competing with Archie for Betty's affections. Adam and Archie don't often get along, but this is mostly because Archie doesn't want Adam to steal Betty away! Betty dated Adam, but Adam once took Ginger Lopez as his date to a dance because Betty was already going with Archie. Betty has been guilty of dating both Archie and Adam in the past… hey, if Archie can do it, so can Betty!

TOÑO DIAZ

First Appearance:
Pal's 'n' Gals Double Digest #123

Toño was born in Mexico and moved to Riverdale after travelling and living all over the country. He loves cooking and dreams of becoming a famous chef when he gets older. Until then, he works with his parents, Adrián and Rosa, for their party planning business. Toño has also been known to use mechanized robots that his father designed to do the gardening, which doesn't always work out well.

SHEILA WU

First Appearance:
Archie & Friends #148, December 2010

Sheila was born in San Francisco to Chinese parents (her father is from Taiwan, her mother is a San Francisco local) and moved to Riverdale at age 9. She's an only child and has a cat named Fluffy. Sheila transferred in from Pine Point High. She loves the color pink so much that she added pink streaks to her long, black hair. She's popular, confident and loves to gossip, but always tries to do right by her friends. Sheila is an extremely fashionable and flashy dresser, often wearing clothes that she has designed and made herself! Her creativity also shines in her activities as a member of the Art Club, the Glee Club, the Prom Decorating Committee and the Yearbook Committee.

AVALON "SHRILL" PRISSTON

First Appearance:
Archie & Friends #148, December 2010

Shrill (don't call her Avalon!) transferred from Pine Point High and keeps her real name highly guarded. She's a goth who loves Heavy and Glam Metal music. She wears deep red contacts and always wears black, sometimes accented with some purple. She's always got on her black lipstick and heavy eyeliner. Shrill makes her own music and is smart, she's a member of the Art Club, the Chess Club, and the Drama Club. Her friends Luce, Denni, and Mob go to another school but they still hang out at the park. Despite her often-intimidating exterior, Shrill has a heart of gold—especially when it comes to her younger sister, Kaylee.

VIC "BIG VIC" JOHNSON

First Appearance:
Archie & Friends #148, December 2010

Big Vic transferred in from Pine Point High. He's a big guy who looks intimidating, but really is quiet and friendly. His favorite subject is math and he's a member of the football team. When he's not on the field, Vic is working part time at his mom's bakery, Mama B's, making decorative cupcakes (and sneaking a few just to taste, too!).

DANNY D'ANGELO

First Appearance:
Archie & Friends #148, December 2010

Danny Transferred to Riverdale from Pine Point High. He's in Band and Music Appreciation Club at school and a member of an amateur rock band after school, writing his own music and playing the guitar. Danny is flirtatious with the girls but also has a goofy side. He likes pranks and joking around, but he is never mean spirited. He rides a motorcycle and likes a grunge clothing style.

BOBBI SUAREZ

First Appearance:
Betty & Veronica #250, December 2010

Bobbi is no-nonsense, confident, and assertive. She knows what she wants and goes for it. She's the editor of the school paper and likes sensational stories that will grab everyone's attention (even if the story isn't fully true). She dresses well and is attractive, but doesn't have time to date, and hasn't had a boyfriend in a while to the disappointment of the guys at Riverdale.

CHLOE MANCUSO

First Appearance:
Archie & Friends #148, December 2010

Chloe transferred to Riverdale from Pine Point High bringing along her intense passion for photography with her! Chloe loves to dig up expose material for the paper and is relentless in her searching. She's outspoken and often speaks before she thinks, which doesn't always end well. Chloe is also very athletic and is on the girls' softball team and the swim team. She's also in the Photography Club and on the Yearbook Committee. Chloe always has her yellow-tinted cat-eye glasses on and has multiple earrings.

CARLA TEAL

First Appearance:
Archie & Friends #148, December 2010

Carla transferred to Riverdale from Pine Point High. She is sight impaired, but that doesn't stop her from anything. Carla is witty and nice and she loves music and dancing, especially with the boys of Riverdale. She's into nature and is an artist, working with ceramics making sculptures.

SHERRY THYME

First Appearance:
Archie #614, December 2010

Sherry is pretty, peppy, and a little vapid. She's friendly with everyone and dates a lot of the boys. She's a member of the Glee Club, Pep Squad, and Prom Committee.

LAWRENCE "LONNIE EASTERMAN" RENWOOD

First Appearance:
Archie & Friends #148, December 2010

Lonnie, as the youngest member of the Renwood family, is insanely rich, but doesn't want to lean on his family's name or wealth. To avoid detection, he goes by "Easterman" so that he can attend the local high school rather than the posh private schools that his older siblings went to. Lonnie is laid back and unimpressed by flashy people, including Veronica. He's smart and his favorite subject is economics. Lonnie is a member of the Basketball Team, Debate Team, and Yearbook Committee and participates in the Student Government.

ROB MONTAUKETT

First Appearance:
Archie #614, December 2010

Rob is Native American and interested in American History. He's not the best student but loves playing sports of any kind, as well as archery. Rob is a bit of a player with the girls, but he's good hearted. He also can have a temper, but is always loyal to his friends.

SAYID JAMAL ALI

First Appearance:
Archie & Friends #148, December 2010

Sayid transferred to Riverdale from Pine Point High and introduced Betty to the new kids. He's friendly with everyone, but keeps his distance from Shrill (who calls him Goose). Sayid is smart, cute, and good at math, though his favorite subject is World History. He's popular and is interested in Betty even though she's with Archie.

CHARLIE "CHUNK" CHARLSTON

First Appearance:
Archie & Friends #149, January 2011

Chunk is a big guy who often has a menacing glare, which keeps kids away from him. He can be rough, but isn't a bully. Despite looking like a mean football player, Chunk is an A student and his favorite subject is Renaissance Literature. He's in the Debate and Drama Clubs and is a member of the Student Government. When he's not studying for school, he enjoys drumming.

SIMON "PRANKENSTEIN" SILVERSTEIN

First Appearance:
Archie #614, December 2010

Simon transferred to Riverdale from Pine Point High. He's a joker and uses the pseudonym Prankenstein to prank the gang, especially Reggie. When he's not causing mayhem, he's studying science, more specifically, oceanography and marine sciences. He mostly keeps to himself, studying marine plants and animals in hopes to develop ecologically sound methods of harvesting seafood and reducing pollution.

THE TWITTERS: MINA, NINA, AND TINA

First Appearance:
Archie #614, December 2010

The Twitters, Mina Martin, Nina Nelson, and Tina Thomas, are all attached at the hip. They finish each other's sentences and dress alike, often wearing white and pink with polka dot or floral patterns. They get stuck on a subject and pursue it relentlessly, unfortunately for Jughead, he caught their attention. They're members of the Glee Club, Prom Committee, and the Yearbook Committee.

NICK ST. CLAIR

First Appearance: *Betty and Veronica Double Digest* #151, July 2007

Nick is a rebel who was kicked out of his old high school in NJ, so his parents sent him to live with his aunt and uncle in Riverdale. Archie and the gang weren't too fond of the unruly Nick, and between his fighting with motorcycle punks, turning in a fake essay, and his penchant for breaking rules, Nick was sent by his parents to Military School. He eventually returned to Riverdale to apologize to the gang, realizing that he had been in the wrong. He uses the catch phrase "A saint I ain't."

SANDRA "SANDY" SANCHEZ

First Appearance: *Jughead's Double Digest Magazine* #140, July 2008

Sandy is a straight-A student and gifted athlete working hard in hopes of getting a college scholarship. Because of her focus on school, she has decided to not date anyone. Sandy does like Jughead, though, and they may have secretly dated at one point!

JUDY JOHNSON

First Appearance: *Archie's Pals 'n' Gals Double Digest Magazine* #125, December 2008

Judy is popular and sociable (with the boys). She dated Moose after he broke up with Midge, which makes her unpopular with Betty, Veronica, and Midge.

PENCILNECK G.

First Appearance: *Archie* #588, October 2008

Pencilneck G is a geek and skateboarder who always has a wool hat pulled down low over his eyes. He's best friends with Zane and friends with Archie. Pencilneck G can get obsessed with things (he particularly likes the TV show *Loss*), which drives the librarian crazy.

ZANE ZAPPAN

First Appearance: *Archie* #590, December 2008

Zane is Pencilneck G's best friend and has a crush on Veronica. He also has Connie and Penelope fighting over him.

JARED MCGERK

First Appearance: *Archie* #588, October 2008

Jared is an upperclassman when Archie was a freshman and is the school bully along with his gang. He's not a good student and is expelled from Riverdale.

WILLIAM

First Appearance:
Veronica #207, August 2011

William is an old friend of Kevin's from Bricktown. William once had a crush on Kevin. He worked with Kevin as a lifeguard during the summer. He was a shaggy kid who turned into a tall, lanky teen with a goatee.

WENDY

First Appearance:
Veronica #207, August 2011

Along with William, they helped Kevin survive his awkward pre-teen years in Bricktown. She and William came out to support Kevin in Riverdale during his performance on the game show *Witmasters*.

DEVON WALTERS

First Appearance:
Kevin Keller #7, March 2013

Devon is Kevin's boyfriend and he loves playing video games. His father lives in Pottstown and wasn't supportive of him being gay (at first). Devon got a taste of notoriety when his and Kevin's kiss went viral (thanks to Veronica) and brought Ellen DeGeneres to town. Devon likes a bit of drama—he pretended to drown at the pool where Kevin was a lifeguard just to get is attention, and he sabotaged a play when Kevin was cast as the lead--but Devon wasn't the lead's love interest!

JERRY

First Appearance:
Veronica #209, December 2011

Jerry is Kevin's old bully and rival. He was a mean kid who was just having trouble at home. He came to see Kevin on *Witmasters* and apologized for his past behavior. Because of his issues at home, Jerry stayed with the Kellers until his aunt could bring him to a safe place.

DEDE DIAZ

First Appearance: *Jughead and Archie Double Digest* #12, July 2015

Dede worked at PEP Comics, a local comic shop owned by her family. She's a fan of comics and a fan of Jughead. Archie asked her out to the movies, and she in turn asked Jughead making it a triple date.

JANUARY MCANDREWS

First Appearance: *Archie Giant Series Magazine* #590, October 1988

January McAndrews, a 29th century descendant of Archie, has the rank of Marshall and is the head of the Time Police. She and Jughead have had an on-again/off-again dating relationship and is possibly the only woman Jughead has loved. She has confessed her love for Jughead, but due to the possible disruption of the time/history balance, they cannot stay together. January is the timekeeper for the Time Policy and spends a lot of her time cleaning up after mistakes that Jughead has made.

AMISHA MEHTA

First Appearance: *Archie* #650, January 2014

Amisha is a Bollywood actress that met Archie in India when The Archies were on their world tour. Amisha and her family moved to Riverdale after meeting Archie. She's a sharp dresser and has eyes for Raj Patel, though Archie has a crush on her (which she doesn't reciprocate). Amisha and Archie teamed up on a Bollywood project for film class.

JINX MALLOY

First Appearance:
Archie's Pal Jughead #135, August 1966

Jinx Malloy is a gloomy, scrawny guy who unknowingly causes calamity wherever he goes. He's scorned by the Riverdale citizens (who try to avoid him), but does find luck with his girlfriend, Lucky Penny. Archie and the Gang use his bad luck on their enemies, but often fall victim to this same bad luck.

RANDOLPH

First Appearance:
Betty & Veronica #180, December 2002

Randolph is a cosmopolitan geek. He loves anime (especially *Captain Tuxedo*) and often walks around with a black top hat, sometimes adding a black cape for dramatic effect. He and Veronica have dated, but he talks a little too much about anime for Veronica's taste and attention span.

GEORGE

First Appearance: *Betty and Veronica* Double Digest #161, July 2008

George was a dating show contestant on *The Lonely Hearts Club* and tried winning Cheryl Blossom's hand. He's a gourmet chef with a goatee and grungy look.

BRANDON

First Appearance: *Betty and Veronica* Double Digest #161, July 2008

Brandon was yet another dating show contestant on *The Lonely Hearts Club*, vying to be Cheryl's suitor. He's an entrepreneur and computer genius, though he's more accident-prone than Archie. By popular audience demand, he won the contest to date Cheryl Blossom.

JAMIE

First Appearance:
Cheryl Blossom #22 May 1999

Jamie is the Blossoms' chauffer, primarily driving Cheryl around town on her shopping sprees. She enjoys working for the family and travels with them on their vacations abroad and is always dressed neatly in her uniform and matching driving cap. Jamie has a secret though… she's psychic! Cheryl had an inkling, but Jamie is keeping this gift to herself to avoid getting roped into opening a Riverdale-based Miss Cleo Psychic Hotline run by Cheryl (who sees dolla dolla bills). Jamie *does* share her gift of being the voice of reason when Cheryl gets a little too outlandish with her outfits or ideas.

PRISCILLA

First Appearance:
Cheryl Blossom #3, November 1995

Priscilla is Cheryl's friend from Pembrooke Academy and though she'll drive her yellow bug to Riverdale to say hi to Cheryl, she prefers to stay in her ultra rich bubble. Priscilla is always well dressed and can usually be found hanging out with fellow super snob, Cedric. Priscilla has a long-time crush on Cheryl's brother Jason, though she instantly had eyes for Jughead (who was oblivious, as always) when she met him at the beach. Not that she'd ever date Jughead for real since Priscilla would never slum it with the Riverdale kids. Just like Cedric, Priscilla is very competitive and will do anything to win.

CEDRIC

First Appearance:
Cheryl Blossom #3, November 1995

Cedric is a friend of Cheryl and Jason's from Pembrooke Academy. Since the Blossoms left, he can be found joined at the hip with Priscilla. Cedric has a bit of a mean streak and is quite the snob, looking down on the people in Riverdale. He did make an exception for Veronica, though, and dated her during the summer (she *may* have had the ulterior motive to gain access to the Pembrooke kids' beach where Archie and Cheryl were hanging out). Just like Priscilla, Cedric is extremely competitive and won't be shown up by the Riverdale gang.

SASSY THRASHER

First Appearance: *Jughead* #30, February 1992

Sassy Thrasher is a tough girl who gets around Riverdale by skateboard as a part of the J-Head Brigade and isn't a fan of Archie or Reggie. Even though she's a skater girl, Sassy is stylish. She's fond of wearing her striped leggings and leather moto vest and keeps her long blond hair pushed back with sunglasses. For a short spell, Sassy worked as a security agent for a local corporation.

For a brief moment (in a story concocted by Jughead for Jellybean), she was a member UGAJ (United Girls Against Jughead) with the other girls of Riverdale.

She also started her own rival girl gang in *Betty & Veronica: Vixens*, called The Thrashers. Her crew consisted of herself, Pepper Smith, Cricket O'Dell, and Sue Stringly.

JOANI JUMPP

First Appearance: *Jughead* #5, April 1988

Joani Jumpp was Jughead's childhood best friend. She moved away when they were in grade school, but came back to Riverdale when her father was transferred. Joani had a crush on Jughead when she was in kindergarten and when she moved back, she found that nothing had changed! She and Jughead picked up where they left off and became fast friends and sometimes dated. Joani and Debbie Dalton are frenemies with both of them vying for Jughead's affections. Joani's dad was transferred to Alaska and as such her whole family had to relocate, but she still comes back to visit Riverdale and Jughead.

DEBBIE DALTON

First Appearance: *Jughead* #5, April 1988

Debbie Dalton moved to Riverdale and immediately caught the attention of Archie and Reggie (and all the other boys!), and she even had Jughead turning his head! Even though they were romantic rivals for Jughead's affection, Debbie and Joanie Jumpp became friends and Debbie eventually broke up with Jughead. Debbie is a fashionable dresser, but has questionable taste in men's clothing (she's a fan of Hawaiian-print neckties?!)

ANITA CHAVITA

First Appearance: *Jughead* #28, December 1991

Anita Chavita is a member of the J-Head Brigade along with Sassy and Jughead. She's in a wheelchair, but that doesn't stop her from grinding the rails! She dated Jughead briefly though she wasn't a fan of his hat and tried to get him to change it (to no avail). Dilton Doiley had a huge crush on Anita and spent his time (too much of it?) trying to break Anita and Jughead up.

GOOGIE GILMORE

First Appearance: *Archie's Pal Jughead Comics* #100, January 1998

Googie Gilmore is Jughead's new neighbor when the Joneses moved to a bigger house in Riverdale. She's everything that Jughead isn't—Googie is well-dressed (she's never without her pearl earrings) and loves bean sprouts and her cat Cleo!

BERNADETTE BROWNIEE

First Appearance: *Archie's Pals 'n' Gals Double Digest Magazine* #135, September 2010

Bernadette Brownlee is the whole package: She's both smart and gorgeous! She's friends with Dilton Doiley and gets along with Archie, but she's more intrigued with Reggie. She has a serious distaste for stand-up comics, but has comebacks for all of Reggie's corny jokes. Reggie can't distract Bernadette too much, though, because she plans on working hard so that she will eventually be President of the United States.

JENNA JACKSON

First Appearance: *Betty and Veronica Comics Digest Magazine* #203, June 2010

Jenna Jackson is a founding member of The Nerd Girls at Riverdale Highschool. She's a fan of studying and getting good grades, but doesn't let that get in the way of her being stylish! She friendly with Betty and invited her to become a member of The Nerd Girls, to Veronica's dismay.

JUANITA

First Appearance: *Betty* #108, March 2002

Juanita is a founding member of The Goodwill Girls along with Betty, Veronica, Tomoko and Nancy and loves helping people. The girls help out around town, making sure the seniors are doing well and working at the soup kitchen.

MAX MARCUS

First Appearance:
Life With Archie (2010 Series) #7, March 2011

Max Marcus is a freshman in Archie's music class and is as much of a troublemaker as Archie was at the same age! He's never without his skateboard and always hangs out with Luke Simon and Soapy Waters. He's been known to cut class and sneak onto campus after hours. Max is a huge music fan with a wide-ranging taste from Jazz to rock. He's a founding member of, and drummer for, the band Riverdale HS band Cheerleader, which is made up of Max (Drums), Georgia (Saxophone), Soapy (Singer), Luke (bass guitar), Lulu (keyboards), and Leroy (guitar). He's keen on making music his life and pushed to get Cheerleader into the Battle of the Bands (with Archie's help). Max has even cut out of a school museum trip to visit Jake's Den, a famous music store.

SOPHIE WATERS

First Appearance:
Life With Archie (2010 Series) #7, March 2011

Sophie "Soapy" Waters is a Freshman at Riverdale Highschool and best friends with Max Marcus and Luke Simon. She's incredibly clumsy, slipping and tripping even over air, hence the nickname "Soapy." She'll do anything to avoid conflict but will also do anything to help her friends, even sneak into the high school when it's closed! Even though she's a klutz, Soapy helped Moose out of Riverdale High School when there was an explosion, saving his life! She's a member of the band Riverdale HS band Cheerleader, which is made up of Max (Drums), Georgia (Saxophone), Soapy (Singer), Luke (bass guitar), Lulu (keyboards), and Leroy (guitar).

LUKE SIMON

First Appearance:
Life With Archie (2010 Series) #7, March 2011

Luke Simon hangs out with Soapy Waters and Max Marcus, bringing up the read when Max causes chaos and catching Soapy when she trips on nothing. He's a bit fashion-challenged and is always in baggie shorts and tees, often mixing patterns (sometimes making it hard to look at him!). He's in dire need of a haircut or barrettes as his long hair is always flopping into his face and hiding his eyes. He's a member of the band Riverdale HS band Cheerleader, where he plays bass guitar.

LULU XU

First Appearance:
Life with Archie (2010 Series) #12, September 2011

Lulu Xu is a Freshman in Archie's music class. She's a great singer, but is happier being in the chorus than in the spotlight. She's also a talented keyboard player and likes playing Jazz music. Lulu is into novels from the '70s and '80s and enjoys reading Kurt Vonnegut. She's a member of the band Riverdale HS band Cheerleader, where she plays keyboards.

JERRY LOPEZ

First Appearance:

Life with Archie (2010 series) #8, April 2011

Jerry Lopez is a friend of Max's and an avid skateboarder. He's a short guy with shaggy brown hair and a skater's sense of style (if the clothes are baggy, he's a fan). Jerry is often the target of Leroy Lodge's teasing and bullying, but has Max to stand up for him. Jerry is very literal with instructions and get distracted a lot in class.

MELONIE

First Appearance:

Life with Archie (2010 series) #10, June 2011

Melonie is a classmate of Max Marcus and is a bit of a rebel, living up to the red hair stereotype! She's not a fan of school and happily cuts out of the museum field trip with Max and Luke Simon to go hang out at the local record shop.

GEORGIA WOLFF

First Appearance:

Life with Archie (2010 series) #9, May 2011

Georgia Wolff is a freshman student of Betty's and a loner. Georgia plays the saxophone and is a big fan of classic Jazz (just look at her giant vinyl and CD collection!). In an effort to not stand out, Georgia wears baggy jeans and a sweatshirt that can swallow her up when she wants to hide. She doesn't talk in class and is often grumpy, but this is just to mask her insecurity about being dyslexic. She's a member of the band Riverdale HS band Cheerleader, where she plays the Saxophone.

THE ADULTS

Riverdale is a sleepy, mid-sized suburban town chock full of places to visit like the movie theater, Pop's Chock'lit Shoppe, and the local parks. The lawns are neat, as are the houses (just don't go into the kids' rooms), and this is thanks to the adults in town keeping the wild kids of Riverdale High School in check. Though it seems like the kids run Riverdale (and maybe they do?!), there are still adults around! There are parents, neighborhood businessowners, and up in the Lodges' neck of town, domestic servants, all trying to keep Archie and the gang in check and teach them how to be the best they can be.

POP TATE

First Appearance:

Pep Comics #46, February 1944

Hair: Balding, Black

Eyes: Brown

Terry "Pop" Tate is the long-time owner of the Chock'lit Shoppe (previously known as Pop's Malt Shop), a diner where Archie and the gang spend most of their time. He's a bit pudgy, thanks to being surrounded by tasty snacks all the time, sports a mustache, has lost most of the hair on his dome (he might blame Jughead for that), and is usually in good spirits. The kids of Riverdale often head to the shop to get advice from Pop, who gladly will listen to the kids and help them out. Pop likes to keep the shop looking retro with a jukebox and old-time ice cream parlor appearance. His biggest customer is Jughead Jones, who has been known to run a significant tab. Pop's cousin Russell owns a similar soda shop in the mountains, but he considers the residents of Riverdale family as well.

FRED ANDREWS

First Appearance:

Pep Comics #22, December 1941

Hair: Balding, Black

Eyes: Brown

Frederick "Fred" Andrews is Archie's dad and husband to Mary Andrews. He's a bit pudgy around the middle and out of shape, though he's strong. Fred is old-fashioned and is often driven mad by Archie's antics, but he's a softie at heart. There's a bit of a generational gap between Fred and his son, but they still bond over shared interests. Fred works as a mid-level manager at a firm that handles industrial automotive sales and is constantly trying to cut down the family's spending, often to no avail.

MARY ANDREWS

First Appearance:

Pep Comics #22, December 1941

Hair: Red

Eyes: Blue

Mary Andrews is Archie's mom and wife to Fred Andrews. She's a typical supermom who was a stay-at-home-mom until she got a job in a real estate agency. Mary doesn't lose her temper, even when Archie gets into trouble (which is often) or doesn't clean his room (can he even find the floor?). She's more tolerant of Archie's behavior than Fred is and is often the only one maintaining order in the house. As much as she loves her family, Mary also enjoys the outdoors and taking long (quiet) solo hikes.

HAL COOPER

First Appearance:

Pep Comics #22, December 1941

Hair: Close crop blond

Eyes: Blue

Hal Cooper is Betty's (sometimes) overprotective father. He's husband to Alice and father to Chic, Polly, and Betty. He's solidly middle-class (and solidly built) and is hard-working pharmacist. Hal introduced Betty to sports and is proud of her achievements as the ultimate cheering dad. He's civic-minded and involved in the local town council and respected by his neighbors. Though Hal supports his daughter, he's also often confused by her antics and doesn't approve of how Archie treats her sometimes.

ALICE COOPER

First Appearance:

Pep Comics #22, December 1941

Hair: short, blond

Eyes: Blue

Alice Cooper is wife to Hal and mother to daughters Betty and Polly and son Chic. She's very close with her girls and is Betty's closest confidante. Alice is the ultimate housewife and warm-hearted. She's proud of Betty and supports her in every endeavor, though she does hope that Betty will outgrow her will outgrow her schoolgirl crush on Archie. Alice is friends with Mary Andrews and Hermione Lodge, though she sometimes envies Hermione's life.

POLLY COOPER

First Appearance: *The Adventures of Little Archie* #23, Summer 1962

Hair: Long, strawberry/honey blond

Eyes: Blue (sometimes has glasses)

Polly Cooper is Betty's smart and metropolitan older sister. She's a television reporter in San Francisco, but makes time to come back to visit her family in Riverdale. Polly is very fashionable and would love to get Betty into some more feminine clothes, but knows what a struggle that would be! There's a bit of an age gap between Polly and her baby sister, so she will sometimes have to take on the role of the adult when their parents aren't available. She loves her life in California, but eventually accepted a television job in Riverdale to be closer to her family.

CHIC COOPER

First Appearance:

Little Archie Mystery #1, August 1963

Hair: Short, strawberry blond

Eyes: Blue

Chic Cooper is Betty's dashing older brother and the eldest Cooper child. He and Polly are a bit older than Betty and he moved out before Betty got to Riverdale High School. He loves his family, but Chic has to keep a low profile as he's a secret agent for the government. Even though he has a serious job, Chic can be a bit of a prankster.

HIRAM LODGE

First Appearance: *Pep Comics* #31, Fall 1942

Hair: Short, neat, white, has a mustache

Eyes: Black/Dark Brown, wears glasses

Hiram Lodge is Veronica's bespectacled father and husband of Hermione. He is a billionaire and a business tycoon, the richest man in Riverdale, and possibly the world! Hiram is the CEO of Lodge Industries. He disapproves of Archie (who has a knack for breaking vases) and has him physically removed from the house often, but puts up with him for Veronica's sake. Even though he's insanely wealthy, Hiram is also a philanthropist and hosts charity events at the Lodge Estate. Hiram is always on the look for new investments, and even when he's sold a garbage dump, he can make it into a profitable ski resort!

HERMIONE LODGE

First Appearance: *Archie Comics* #37, March-April 1949

Hair: Short, white

Eyes: Blue

Hermione Lodge is Veronica's mother and wife to Hiram. She's a very elegant, willowy woman who clearly has passed her sense of style down to her daughter. Hermione is never without her pearls and is a blue-blood through and through. Although she is the richest woman in Riverdale and doesn't need to work, Hermione is active in her women's social group and loves participating in philanthropic organizations, especially when it means throwing a charity gala at the Lodge Estate.

HUBERT SMITHERS

First Appearance: *Archie's Pals 'n' Gals* (1952 series) #1, October 1952

Hair: Short, black, balding on top

Eyes: Black/Dark Brown

Hubert Smithers, or just Smithers for short, is the butler/majordomo for the Lodge household. His father was also a butler for the Lodge family and Smithers was childhood friends with Hiram (who called him Smitty). Smithers is a rotund man, but is strong enough to physically eject Archie and Jughead from the Lodge residence when needed (which is often). He takes his job very seriously and is always dressed formally, often in a tuxedo and waistcoat. Smithers is unflappable except when Veronica's friends come over and start wreaking havoc around the house!

GASTON

First Appearance: *Archie Giant Series Magazine* #11, June 1961

Hair: Short, Black, pencil mustache

Eyes: Black

Gaston is the Lodge family chef and takes his work very seriously. He's tall and skinny with a pencil-thin mustache and thick French accent. Gaston is a professionally-trained French chef who is often driven mad by Jughead's less-than-sophisticated palate, though Jughead will eat anything Gaston prepares. Gaston considers the kitchen his domain and would prefer if everyone (even Veronica) would stay out of it.

FORSYTHE PENDLETON JONES, JR.

First Appearance: *Archie Comics* #16, Fall 1945

Hair: black, balding, mustache

Eyes: Black/Dark Brown

Forsythe Pendleton Jones, Jr. is husband to Gladys and father to Jughead and Jellybean. He works for the city in park maintenance and provides a good life for his family, though he is sometimes prone to be as lazy as his son. Forsythe is a skinny, balding man but was athletic as a teen and wishes his son would follow suit. Now, the closest he gets to sports is watching them on TV and snacking like an athlete. He's a hard worker, but sometimes has money trouble, which is not helped when Jellybean manages to get ahold of and throw out his paycheck!

GLADYS JONES

First Appearance: *Archie Comics* #20, 1946

Hair: short, black

Eyes: Black/Dark Brown

Gladys Jones is Forsythe's wife and mother to Jughead and Jellybean. She has a sister (Wilma Wilkin) and a brother (Herman). Like her husband and son, Gladys is tall and skinny. She is a stay-at-home-mom and her goal in life is to get some ambition into her son so he'll do his chores without her telling him to. She's friends with Hermione Lodge and Alice Cooper and active around Riverdale when not chasing after Jellybean and Jughead.

COL. THOMAS KELLER

First Appearance:

Veronica #209, December 2011

Hair: Short, silver sides, light brown top

Eyes: Blue

Retired US Army Colonel Thomas Keller is husband to Kathy and dad to Denise, Patty, and Kevin. He spent three decades in the Army and sometimes has a little trouble forgetting he's a civilian. He wants the best for his children and encourages Kevin to pursue any career path, even if it's not in the military. When he realized Kevin was The Equalizer, he was eager to train him in combat. Colonel Keller is a stern, but loving man and when he met his wife, Kathy, in college, was too nervous to speak with her so he wrote her love notes (which she still keeps!).

KATHERINE KELLER

First Appearance:

Veronica #209, December 2011

Hair: Mid-length, layered, bright red

Eyes: Blue

Katherine Keller, better known as Kathy, is wife to Colonel Thomas Keller and mom to Denise, Patty, and Kevin. She is the ultimate Mama Bear, sometimes called "Grizzly Mama" by her husband because she's so protective of her family. If anyone wants to come after any of her kids, they will have to pass through her first (spoiler alert, they won't get past her). To balance out her "Grizzly" side, Kathy also practices yoga to center herself and teaches yoga in Riverdale.

REGINALD MANTLE JR.

First Appearance: *Pep Comics* #52, March 1945

Reginald "Ricky" Mantle, Jr. is married to Vicky Mantle and father to Reggie and Oliver Mantle, though sometimes he'd like to disown Reggie. Ricky is the owner and Editor in Chief of the local Riverdale newspaper, *The Riverdale Gazette*, as well as owner of the newspaper publishing company which owns the Gazette. He's a Type-A personality and was a football star back in his high school days. Ricky enjoys playing poker with his friends and hunting down the next big news story. Often his drive to work means he neglects his son, but they became closer after Ricky had a heart attack and was laid up in the hospital, forcing Reggie to take over the newspaper for a spell. The Mantles are upper middle-class, but not quite as wealthy as the Lodges.

VICTORIA MANTLE

First Appearance: *Archie's Rival Reggie* #6, July 1952

Vicky Mantle is Ricky's wife and Reggie and Oliver's mother. She fully enjoys being a housewife and spends her afternoons lunching with her country club friends. Vicky is quick to support charities, but sometimes will neglect to support her son. She loves Reggie, but has difficulty being there for him. Vicky enjoys planning charity events and playing tennis at the club.

OLIVER MANTLE

First Appearance: *Life With Archie* #26, March 2013

Oliver Mantle is Reggie's younger brother, and son to Ricky and Vicky. He got out of Riverdale as soon as he could and moved as far away as he could so he could live in the wilds of Alaska. Like his father, Oliver is a reporter, but he doesn't have the same hunger for the business, his passion is the great outdoors and while he loves his family, he has no intention of ever running *The Riverdale Gazette*.

CLIFFORD BLOSSOM

First Appearance:

Cheryl Blossom #1, September 1995

Hair: Short, auburn red, mustache/beard

Eyes: Brown

Clifford Blossom is married to Penelope Blossom and father to Cheryl and Jason. The Blossoms are wealthier than the Lodges, thanks to Clifford's success as a software designer and owner of multiple companies (including USA Media, the company Cheryl once sued, not knowing her dad owned it. Whoops—hey, that's a mistake anyone could make!). After a bad business decision, his company went bankrupt, but Hiram Lodge bought it out, saving the Blossom family from becoming poor. Clifford is a shrewd businessman and talented software designer, but he also is a little cagey when it comes to hiding the family's assets. After all of the family's ups and downs, it's revealed that Clifford is not Cheryl and Jason's biological dad.

PENELOPE BLOSSOM

First Appearance:

Cheryl Blossom #1, September 1995

Hair: Short, wavy, bright red

Eyes: Blue

Penelope Blossom is married to Clifford and mom to Cheryl and Jason. She lives the life of an upper-class woman, spending her time at the country club lunching with her friends and planning charity events. She's a kind woman who wants the best for her family and Riverdale.

EDUARDO LOPEZ

First Appearance: *Betty and Veronica Spectacular* #50, November 2001

Hair: Short, Dark brown, goatee/mustache

Eyes: Brown

Eduardo Lopez is a world-famous chef and is married to Gloria Lopez and father to Ginger, Teresa, and Eliza. He had a restaurant in New York City and decided to branch out by opening a new restaurant in Riverdale, moving his family along with him. Eduardo is well known from his appearances on The Cooking Network and is a happy, even-keeled guy (unlike some other chefs on the network!).

GLORIA LOPEZ

First Appearance: *Betty and Veronica Spectacular* #50, November 2001

Hair: Long, auburn (braided)

Eyes: Brown, glasses

Gloria Lopez is married to Eduardo and mom to Ginger, Teresa, and Eliza. When her family moved from NYC to Riverdale for Eduardo's new restaurant, she took a job at the Riverdale Zoo. Like her husband, Gloria is well-known from her work on television—she's an animal trainer and expert who brings her furry (and sometimes scaly) friends onto television programs. She's just as happy being home cooking with her family as she is showing off the zoo's collection, though!

RAVI PATEL

First Appearance:

Tales from Riverdale Digest #21, August 2007

Hair: Short, silver sides, black on top, mustache

Eyes: Brown, glasses

Dr. Ravi Patel is married to Mona Patel and father to Raj and Tina. When his family moved to Riverdale, he opened a small office attached to his house, Ravi Patel, MD Family Practice. He is a serious and fastidious man who doesn't need a cuff to tell that Raj makes his blood pressure rise! He sees a lot of himself in daughter Tina, but can't quite figure out why Raj is obsessed with movies (or why he can't stay out of trouble). Even though he's a bit severe, Dr. Patel is always kind to his family and patients.

MONA PATEL

First Appearance:

Tales from Riverdale Digest #21, August 2007

Hair: Long, Black, braided down back

Eyes: Brown

Mona Patel is married to Dr. Ravi Patel and mother to Raj and Tina. She's a research scientist but has a bit more humor about Raj's antics than her husband does. She's well-respected in her field and works hard, but is also a loving mother who is involved in her children's lives. Raj sometimes tests her patience, but she knows that some experiments have unexpected (and sometimes explosive) outcomes!

ARTIE ANDREWS

First Appearance:
Pep Comics #23, January 1942
Hair: Short, fading red
Eyes: Blue

Artie Andrews is Archie's paternal grandfather. Archie definitely takes after him with the red hair, freckles, and penchant for getting into trouble. Artie is calmer now, but got into plenty of scrapes as a kid and loves to talk about them. He's married to Bernice (who looked a lot like Betty when she was in Riverdale High School), and his partner in crime during his teen years was Curly (who bore a striking resemblance to Jughead). Artie is always dressed smartly in checkered slacks, a sweater vest, and a bowtie. Though he was a bit of a trouble-magnet in his youth, he also went out of his way to help those in need, which once included a young Hiram Lodge who was visiting Riverdale and got lost (multiple times).

UNCLE HERMAN

First Appearance: *Archie's Pal Jughead* #1 (1949)
Hair: Shaggy, white, mustache (Wilkin stories)
(Black, bald on top – first appearance)
Eyes: Black, glasses

Uncle Herman is Wilma Wilkin and Gladys Jones' brother, making him Jughead and Bingo's uncle. He's a rotund man who is incapable of staying out of trouble. He played professional baseball when he was younger (known by the nickname Rabbit back then). Uncle Herman cannot stop tinkering with electronics, which often leaves a trail of destruction. Along with electronics, he also invents potions and pretty much anything else his scattered brain can think of!

MR. WALDO WEATHERBEE

First Appearance: *Jackpot Comics* #5, Spring 1942

Hair: Bald (with a few stragglers holding on the top)

Eyes: Black, glasses

Mr. Waldo Weatherbee is Riverdale High School's beloved principal. He's a rotund man and has a twin brother, Tony, and niece Wendy Weatherbee. He became principal of Riverdale High School right as Archie and the gang started their freshman year. Perhaps he can handle Archie because as a student at Riverdale High School (way back when), he was a bit of a troublemaker, even claiming the nickname "Wild Wally" from classmate Fred Andrews. Even though the kids get into his non-existent hair all the time, he is fond of them and tries to teach Archie and his friends life lessons (which stick sometimes).

MS. GERALDINE GRUNDY

First Appearance:
Jackpot Comics #4, Winter 1941

Hair: White, wears a low bun

Eyes: Blue

Ms. Geraldine Grundy is Riverdale High School's teacher extraordinaire. She has taught pretty much every class that Riverdale has to offer. She's a tall, skinny woman with a prominent nose and always has her hair in a low bun. She grew up in Riverdale and dated Mr. Weatherbee when they were in high school and they remain friends as educators. Before she became a teacher she worked at a pickle-packing plant and served with the Women's Army Corps (WACs) during WWII. She cares for her students and is always pushing them to do their best. She's not often caught up in the gang's pranks since she can see right through them and sidestep any disaster.

PROF. FLUTESNOOT

First Appearance:
Archie's Pal Jughead #1, 1949

Professor Benjamin Flutesnoot is Riverdale
High School's resident science teacher and
lives up to his name with a nose you can't
miss. He's a bit of a mad scientist and often
singes his white lab coat from an experiment
gone wrong. He's friendly with Mr. Weatherbee and Ms. Grundy and has
mistaken Mr. Svenson's scrambled radio for alien transmissions. As well as
being the science teacher, he's also the music teacher, though most of the
students in his class are tone deaf. Who knows, maybe he can create a potion
to give the kids musical ears?

MISS BEAZLY

First Appearance:
Pep Comics #93, September 1952

Miss Bernice Beazly is the ever-present
cafeteria cook at Riverdale High School,
though "cook" might be a bit of a strong
word for it. Her meals are notoriously bad,
though Jughead is a fan of her cooking
and, as such, Jughead is one of the few people she appreciates. Miss Beazly's
hair is always living its own life, sticking out everywhere, frizzled and white,
from beneath her cook's cap. Though the students and faculty don't love her
cooking, she has won blue ribbons in competitions for her Fiesta dish. She's
friendly with Mr. Svenson, but that's about it—everyone else (especially Mr.
Weatherbee) should clear a wide path around her as she has no fear about
expressing her loud, surly, and sarcastic thoughts to anyone.

MR. SVENSON

First Appearance:
Archie's Joke Book Magazine #35, July 1958

Mr. Svenson is Riverdale High School's janitor
and speaks with a heavy Swedish accent.
He's a hard worker and does his job well, but
isn't the brightest bulb in the supply closet—he
misinterprets instructions occasionly which
leads to a bit of confusion all around. He's friendly with the students at
Riverdale and with Ms. Beazly and can be heard exclaiming "By Yiminy!"
whenever he's excited.

COACH KLEATS

First Appearance:
Pep Comics #24, February 1942

Coach Kleats is Riverdale High School's head
coach and gym teacher. He used to be a great
athlete in his youth, but now he'd rather lead
than compete himself. He may have lost his
athleticism, but he didn't lose his drive to win! He's
always pushing the kids to play their strongest
and win against their rivals.

COACH CLAYTON

First Appearance:
Laugh Comics #244, July 1971

Coach Floyd Clayton is married to Alice Clayton
and dad to Chuck. He's Coach Kleats' assistant
and actually looks like he could jump in and
play in a game. As well as being a coach, he's
a gym teacher at Riverdale High School and is
a teacher that the kids go to with their problems. He's firm and always
trying to get the kids to work out, but he also listens to their problems
and offers solutions.

MS. PHLIPS

First Appearance:
Archie and Me #15, June 1967
Hair: Short, black
Eyes: Brown

Ms. Phlips is Mr. Weatherbee's secretary and could be the reason the school doesn't go into absolute chaos on a daily basis. She's prim and neat and is friendly with all of the teachers at Riverdale High School. She's calm and reliable and often acts as a liaison between the students and the staff.

V.P. SANCHEZ

First Appearance:
Archie #521, June 2002
Hair: Short, curly, Dark Brown (almost black)
Eyes: Brown [has a mole on her right cheekbone]

Rita Sanchez was hired to be Weatherbee's Vice Principal and very quickly started turning the school around. She set up an arts exhibition room for the kids to express themselves and has open conversations with the kids about how Riverdale High School can be improved. Vice Principal Sanchez is always dressed smartly in a pantsuit or skirt suit and is never without her glasses atop her curly hair. In addition to adding programs and incentives for the kids to get better grades, she upgraded the school cafeteria and menu. She's incredibly organized and doesn't always see eye to eye with Mr. Weatherbee but they always come to an agreement. Vice Principal Sanchez can't figure out how to handle Archie, which is good news for Mr. Weatherbee otherwise he'd be out of a job due to VP Sanchez's extreme competence!

V.P. HOWITZER

First Appearance: *Archie at Riverdale High* #100, December 1984

Vice Principal Patton Howitzer (yes, like the tank) is a former drill sergeant who rules Riverdale High School with an iron fist. He's war-obsessed and possibly the meanest teacher to walk the halls of the high school. VP Howitzer is a former Marine and can't stop acting like one, even down to still wearing his military uniform, hat and all, and making the kids to pushups when they're "insubordinate." He filled in temporarily for Mr. Weatherbee as the principal when Mr. Weatherbee hurt his back playing football with the team (don't ask) and turned Riverdale HS into a boot camp, which was not popular with the students. After his stint at substitute principal, he stayed on as VP and toned down the drill sergeant persona (just a smidge).

SUPERINTENDENT HASSLE

First Appearance: *Archie and Me* #64, April 1974

Superintendent Hassle oversees the Riverdale school system and makes Mr. Weatherbee nervous with his unannounced drop-ins, but they ultimately get along as they both have the kids' best interests at heart. Superintendent Hassle is always dressed well in his suit and hat and comes across as a bit angry and brusque, but down inside he's a friendly guy and is impressed by the way Riverdale HS runs and the kids and staff there.

MISS HAGGLY

First Appearance:
Laugh Comics #50, April 1952
Hair: White hair with curls at the side
Eyes: Brown

Miss Haggly is the oldest and longest-serving teacher at Riverdale High School (and looks it). She's a little portly and has wrinkles, but she's always dressed well, often wearing clothing with ruffles around the neck and sleeves. She teaches history and at times seems a little out of touch, but like her friend Ms. Grundy, isn't often bothered by the students' antics and is able to keep current with what they're talking about.

MR. GRIMLEY

First Appearance: *Archie at Riverdale High* #108, April 1986
Hair: Short, curly, black w/ mustache
Eyes: Brown, glasses

Mr. Putnam Grimley took over as Riverdale High School's guidance counselor. He dresses a bit drably and his office is a bit of a mess, but he does try to help the students. He sits down with the students to discuss their future plans and careers, but these conversations often leave him more stressed than ever. Mr. Grimley couldn't handle the stress of being a guidance counselor and switched to become the Driver's Ed teacher, which was possibly the worst move he could have made as that was even MORE stressful!

PRINCIPAL STANGER

First Appearance: *Jughead* #1, December 2015

Principal Stanger took over at Riverdale High School following Mr. Weatherbee's forced early retirement. Jughead suspected him to be a C.R.U.S.H. Agent because of his new, strict policies and use of drones to keep an eye on the students. It turned out that Principal Stanger is a disgraced former spy who was downgraded to the CIA's training department to oversee the publishing of their manuals. He's been lying to his bosses, claiming he was looking for printing plants when in reality he was gathering data on the students in an attempt to find trainee spies. Thankfully Hiram Lodge brought in the authorities and had him arrested before a student spy army could be created!

COACH ENG

First Appearance: *Jughead* #2, January 2016

Coach Eng was the new gym teacher at Riverdale High School and came in at the same time as Principal Stanger. The two of them are friends and hold a special contempt for Jughead as he seems to be immune to their wrath. It turned out that Coach Eng's courses were actually training and testing tools for Principal Stanger's student-spy recruitment program (which luckily is cut down by Mr. Lodge before any real damage was done!).

MS. MCCONE

First Appearance: *Jughead* #3, February 2016

Ms. McCone (or if you ask Archie, Ms. McDrone) was the new science teacher at Riverdale High Schoolr. She was a part of the teacher shake-up at Riverdale HS and ran the new drone program, making the students assemble the drones that were then used to then surveil them. She departed Riverdale HS when Principal Stanger was arrested and replaced.

MR. ISAAC M. FINE

First Appearance:
Archie #614, December 2010
Hair: Short, wavy, white
Eyes: Brown, glasses
Hobbies: Birdwatching

Mr. Fine moved to teach at Riverdale when
Pine Point High School closed. He's a math
teacher and will take any opportunity to argue with Professor Flutesnoot about which is better: math or science. Mr. Fine is a dapper dresser and once he sees Ms. Grundy for the first time, is smitten with her.

MS. AMANDA ASHTON

First Appearance:
Archie #614, December 2010
Hair: Large/thick locs, dark reddish-brown
Eyes: Brown, glasses

Mrs. Ashton also moved to teach at Riverdale
when Pine Point High School closed. Back at
Pine Point, she was the head of the English
Department and had big plans for it. She was also in line to be the Vice Principal at Pine Point before they closed, leaving her possibly with an eye toward the same position at Riverdale. Mrs. Ashton is always dressed well and in bright colors, which goes right along with her bright glasses!

MS. KAMINI GANESH

First Appearance:
Archie & Friends #148, December 2010
Hair: Long, straight, black
Eyes: Brown

Ms. Ganesh was another transfer to Riverdale
from Pine Point High School. She's a world
traveler with lots of stories to tell! She teaches
Geography and World History. Ms. Ganesh has
a Bindi on her forehead and likes to wear bright colors.

MS. PETRA LAURIETTE

First Appearance:
Jughead's Double Digest #165, January 2011
Hair: Long, straight, black
Eyes: Blue, glasses

Ms. Lauriette was brought in to Riverdale
HS to head up the new Arts and Education
program, which combined Drama and
Literature. She's a teacher who's passionate about poetry and classic literature
and wants to inspire the kids to love it as well. The boys may not care at
all about poetry or plays, but they're definitely smitten by the beautiful Ms.
Lauriette (especially Reggie)! She tapped Jughead to play Cyrano de Bergerac
for the class's reading of the play and impressed Principal Weatherbee with the
final production.

"MAMA B" JOHNSON

First Appearance: *Betty* #189, February 2011

Mama B is Bic Vic Johnson's mother and
the proprietor and main baker at Mama B's
Bakery in Riverdale. She's a strong woman
who opened the bakery before Vic was born
and made it a staple in Riverdale. She loves
to experiment with cupcake flavors and loves
having Vic working beside her in the shop, even though he slacks off at
times to chat with friends!

SEGARINI

First Appearance: *Archie's Pal Jughead
Comics* #128, July 2000

Segarini owns the local pizza shop in
Riverdale and is Pop Tate's biggest rival.
They're constantly battling it out for best
hangout for the kids, but Archie and his gang
are loyal to Pop's (though Jughead is a fan).
Segarini will give you a free pizza if you beat him at arm wrestling, but he's
a pretty strong guy from tossing pizzas all day!

DR. CLAY WALKER

First Appearance:
Life with Archie #16, February 2012

Dr. Clay Walker is Kevin Keller's husband and
runs a medical clinic in Riverdale. He was Kevin's
physical therapist at the VA Hospital where Kevin
recovered from serious injuries he sustained while
serving overseas. Clay is always trying to help
everyone and when trying to intervene in a robbery at Jo's auto shop, he was
shot. Recovery was long, but with Kevin's help, Clay fully recovered.

FRED MIRTH

First Appearance:
Life with Archie #1, September 2010

Fred owns the country's largest investment banking
firm. He and Ethel Muggs were once engaged, but
Fred's focus on buying up Riverdale properties proved
too much for Ethel and the engagement was called
off. When Veronica and Archie found out about Fred's plans to bulldoze parts of
town, Fred framed Veronica, and skipped town. Eventually Veronica cleared her
name and provided proof of Fred's misdeeds which led to his imprisonment.

JO JOBANPOTRA

First Appearance: *Life with Archie* #8, March 2011

Jo Jobanpotra owns Jo's Garage, the local auto
shop where Reggie worked and is a talented
mechanic. Her shop was held up at gunpoint
during a rash of robberies around Riverdale but
Dr. Clay Walker jumped in and redirected the
gunman's focus. Jo tolerates the cameras that
follow Reggie around for the reality TV series Betty Loves
Reggie, but she'd much rather be left a lone to work on engines.

MOE MILLER

First Appearance:
Life with Archie #4, December 2010

Moe "Moe the Maven" Miller is a restaurant
franchise salesman that Archie ran into at
the Franchise Expo in Las Vegas. Moe is
constantly looking for a deal and coming up
with wacky new restaurant ideas. Moe thinks
Jughead makes the best burger he's ever tasted and convinces Jughead to
franchise the Chocklit Shoppe and brings in investors which helps keep the
restaurant afloat.

SIMON CRIKEY

First Appearance:
Life with Archie #15,
January 2012

Simon Crikey is
the cranky British
producer for the reality show Betty
Loves Reggie. He's good at his
job, but can't help but amp up
the excitement at all times, even
if that means creating a fictional
reality for Betty and Reggie. When
Reggie and Betty pushed back
on creating fake drama, Simon
pivoted to a new type of meta-TV:
a reality show ABOUT a reality
show.

ILANA ROBBINS

First Appearance:
Life with Archie #1,
September 2010

Ilana Robbins is
Moose's (or Duke,
as she calls him) girlfriend and
has helped him get control of his
temper. She practices yoga and
meditation and even gave Moose
a dog (Sam) to help him relax
during his run for Riverdale's
mayor. She is legally blind,
but that doesn't stop her from
engaging in the activities she
loves, nor does it prevent her from
living her life to the fullest.

SHIRA

First Appearance:
Life with Archie #1,
September 2010

Shira is Archie and
Betty's neighbor in
New York City. She is a film editor
and production partner with Amy
Learsi on the movie Mr. Justice.
Shira loves life in the city and is
always looking for the next story
to turn into a blockbuster movie.
She's a big comics fan (especially
Mr. Justice) and an even bigger
fan of Alexis Click, another friend
of Betty and Archie.

AMY LEARSI

First Appearance:
Life with Archie #1,
September 2010

Amy Learsi is Shira's
production partner
on the movie Mr. Justice and lives
in the same apartment building
in NYC as Archie and Betty.
When the original composer for
Mr. Justice dropped out, Amy
hired Archie to score the film.
Unfortunately, she was unable to
fight for Archie when the original
composer came waltzing back in
and demanded his job back.

ALEXIS CLICK

First Appearance:
Life with Archie #1,
September 2010

Alexis Click is a
friend of Archie
and Betty's in NYC and lives in
the same apartment building as
them. She has a popular daily
news show on TV called Click on
Alexis. She's always hunting the
hot stories whether they're about
the latest celebrity wedding (or
divorce) or a corporate takeover.
Alexis works hard but also loves
spending time with her kids, who
are huge Mr. Justice fans.

IAN DUNCAN

First Appearance:
Life with Archie #1,
September 2010

Ian Duncan is the
"Best actor on or off
Broadway." Or at least he is if you
ask Betty! Ian is a neighbor and
friend of Archie and Betty in NYC
and is a working actor. He loves
being on stage, but wouldn't say
no if Shira and Amy were to cast
him in the next superhero movie
they produce!

ARIEL ST. CLAIR

First Appearance:
Life with Archie #1,
September 2010

Ariel St. Clair is a
friend and neighbor
of Archie and Betty in NYC and
is the city's hottest contemporary
sculptor. When Sack's Sixth
Avenue cut Betty's pay and
eventually laid her off, Ariel hired
her on as a part time art agent.
Betty helped get Ariel an in at
the prestigious Elkind Gallery but
Ariel's work speaks for itself and
she always has a steady stream
of commissions from clients.

"BIG" MIKE SINGER

First Appearance:
Life with Archie #1,
September 2010

Big Mike Singer is
a friend of Archie
and Betty's in NYC, though he's
not often around long enough to
hang out. He's an imposing figure,
always dressed in a dark suit,
earpiece, and black sunglasses.
He claims to be a CIA agent,
which is believable to Archie and
Betty since Mike will disappear for
weeks at a time. He's a mystery
wrapped in an enigma wearing a
dark suit.

DAPHNE WELLER

First Appearance:
Life with Archie #22,
June 2012

Daphne Weller is Betty's assistant at her catering company, Cuisine by Betty. Daphne looks like Betty's polar opposite with black and purple hair, multiple piercings (lips, ears, eyebrow), and ripped fishnets, but she admires Betty and they get along great! Daphne loves the spotlight and has no problem being a part of Betty Loves Reggie, their reality TV show.

DAVEY LARSEN

First Appearance:
Life with Archie #25,
February 2013

Davey Larsen was Jellybean's boyfriend who showered her with affection, but always seemed to be bad news. He tried to convince Jellybean into leaving Jughead's Chocklit Shoppe unlocked one night. Jellybean knew better, though, and tipped her brother and the authorities off—good thing, too as Davey was one of the crew involved with robbing businesses all over Riverdale!

DAVE KLONSKY

First Appearance:
Life with Archie #26,
January 2013

Dave Klonksy works with Dr. Wannamaker and had the unfortunate pleasure of being Dr. Clay Walker's physical therapist after Clay was shot defending Jo Jobanpotra against the robber. Dave is a kind and patient man, which came in handy when Clay thought he knew better after his one rotation on the physical therapy ward. Dave is good at his job, though, and eventually helped Clay get back on his feet (literally!).

GARETH MCGRAW

First Appearance:
Life with Archie #26,
January 2013

Gareth McGraw is one of the producers at Mirth Music. He works with Sheila and Eric making radio hits and wasn't so sure Archie was the right man to head up the label when Fred Mirth brought him in. Gareth knows his hits, though, and helped get Archie up to speed even though he didn't agree with bringing in unknown talent.

SHEILA WATSON

First Appearance:
Life with Archie #26, January 2013

Sheila Watson is a producer at Mirth Music and had little confidence in Archie when Fred Mirth brought him in as president of the label. Like Gareth McGraw and Eric Nostrand, her co-producers, she focuses her effort on known entities and cranking out radio-friendly music. Even though she didn't totally trust that Archie is up for the job, she still helped Archie find his feet in the business.

ERIC NOSTRAND

First Appearance:
Life with Archie #26, January 2013

Eric Nostrand is a producer at Mirth Music and like his co-producers Gareth McGraw and Sheila Watson, had little confidence in Archie when Fred Mirth brought him in as president of the label. Eric knows how to work the sound board and make mediocre musicians and songs sound award-worthy.

SHARON ROPER

First Appearance:
Life with Archie #28, May 2013

Sharon Roper was Veronica's assistant and *seemed* to be a perfect fit for Lodge and Associates, but she was really a saboteur planted by Fred Mirth. Sharon helped plant evidence in Veronica's office that implicated Veronica in shady bribes to government officials. Sharon was a gifted grifter and escaped with Fred on his private jet as the FBI raided Veronica's office.

KEITH DIAMOND

First Appearance:
Life with Archie #26, January 2013

Keith Diamond is a true gem of a man. He was hired by Veronica to be the media coordinator for the CBBCF, Cheryl Blossom's foundation. He has movie star looks and was immediately taken with Cheryl, asking her to dinner after their first introduction! Keith also jumped straight into the job of promoting awareness about breast cancer and getting Cheryl onto TV talk shows to discuss her diagnosis.

LOUISE HARKINS

First Appearance:
Life with Archie #27,
April 2013

Louise Harkins,
a retired biology
professor from State U, lives in
Hartsburg but ran into Waldo
Weatherbee while hiking in
Riverdale. She's an avid birdwatcher
and is uncanny in her bird call
mimicking. Like Waldo, she lost
her spouse and retired from an
academic job. She volunteers and
keeps busy around town. She and
Waldo dated and of course she said
yes when he proposed!

RITA LOVELY

First Appearance:
Life with Archie #20,
June 2012

Nurse Rita Lovely
works with Dr. Clay
Walker in Dr. Barnes' clinic. She's
friendly and a great nurse, but has
absolutely no tolerance for Simon
Crikey and his camera crew.
Rita takes her job seriously and
protects her patients' privacy at
all costs. When she's not working,
Rita had her nose buried in
mystery novels trying to figure out
"whodunit."

J.J. HARMON

First Appearance:
Life with Archie #3,
July 2013

J.J. Harmon is a
criminal defense
attorney who represented Veronica
after Fred Mirth set her up. He's a
shark in the courtroom and wins
any case he tries, but he also cares
about his clients and treats them as
if they were his own family. When
he's not defending wrongfully-
accused clients, he relaxes by
baking fine French pastries (which
he may taste a little too often for his
doctor's liking!).

WENDELL SIMMONS

First Appearance:
Life with Archie #32,
November 2013

Wendell Simmons
was an unassuming
newcomer to Riverdale who started
working at Jughead's Chocklit
Shoppe. He's a quiet guy but
harbors a deep bigotry against
Kevin Keller. Wendell pulled out a
gun during Kevin's post-fundraiser
party at the Chocklit Shoppe and
attempted to assassinate Kevin.
Archie jumped in front of his friend,
taking the bullet himself. Wendell
was taken into custody.

NICK ELROY

First Appearance:
Life with Archie #32,
November 2013

Nick Elroy took on the daunting job of manager at Chowhouse Too when Ambrose reopened the venue. Nick moved to Riverdale from NYC after getting burned out from the grind. Nick knows how to manage a business and renegotiated with all of Ambrose's vendors, sometimes to Archie's dismay. His laser focus on tightening the reigns could definitely be tied to his past as a Master Sergeant in the Army.

MIKE BAKER

First Appearance:
Life with Archie #34,
April 2014

Mike Baker moved to Riverdale and found work as the new security guard at Chowhouse Too. He's a quiet guy and keeps to himself, but he hit it off with Nick Elroy, the venue's new manager. Mike is hyper observant and quick on his feet, though not quick enough to prevent Archie from getting shot. Mike did tackle the shooter, though, and subdued him so no one else could get hurt.

GWEN GILES

First Appearance:
Life with Archie #34,
April 2014

Gwen Giles is another of Fred Mirth's associates and almost went into business with Veronica on the phony Riverhart Project. Gwen represented a financial syndicate and likes living the rich life. But when Veronica planted a bug in her house, Gwen almost immediately incriminated herself and gave up Fred's location so the authorities were able to arrest both of them which led to Veronica's exoneration.

THE KIDDIES AND THE PETS!

Archie and his friends aren't the only trouble makers in Riverdale! The town has plenty of kids creating mischief while Archie is chasing Betty and Veronica and Jughead is chasing a burger. And what's life without furry friends?! Riverdale has plenty of pets running around or helping their owners out of pickles.

AMBROSE PIPPS

First Appearance: *Little Archie* #4, Fall 1957

Ambrose Pipps was a small kid who could usually be found trailing Archie and the gang when they were little kids. His oversized baseball cap was always pulled down over his eyes, but somehow he always found Archie. Ambrose was constantly trying to impress Archie, who wanted none of it. The two became friends when Ambrose moved back to Riverdale as a teen and Archie apologized for his past behavior. In *Life with Archie*, Ambrose owns The Chowhouse II, a diner that Archie helped him revamp into a club/music venue. In *Vixens*, Ambrose owns Ambrose's Mechanics, the shop Betty and Veronica's gang called home base and went to get their motorcycles tuned up. Ambrose and his girlfriend Bubbles McBounce could fix up any car or motorcycle and stood their ground against rival gangs like Fangs Fogarty's Serpents.

EVELYN EVERNEVER

First Appearance: *Little Archie* #4, Fall 1957

Evelyn Evernever was a shy girl who hung around with Archie and his friends when they were children. Her only real friend was her doll, Minerva. Although she was shy, Evelyn thought of herself as "a bou'tiful gal" and could come out of her shell when she needed to teach Archie a lesson. And don't tell Betty or Veronica, but Evelyn was Archie's first kiss! As a member of Betty and Veronica's gang, the *Vixens*, Evelyn is a bit of a wild card. She has a quarter-sleeve Minerva tattoo on her right arm and a scar on her right cheek. No one really knows where she was during her absence from Riverdale and Evelyn isn't keen on sharing. She's mysterious and tough as nails, often going rogue and antagonizing both friends and enemies.

FANGS FOGARTY

First Appearance:
Little Archie #56, November 1969

Fred "Fangs" Fogarty was Archie's childhood bully and got his name from his prominent snaggletooth. Even though Fangs would go out of his way to pick on most of the kids in school, he appointed Penny Peabody as his girlfriend. Fangs moved out of Riverdale and came back for a visit as a changed man. His attitude was greatly improved, as were his teeth and nickname.

In *Vixens*, Fangs Fogarty was the leader of The Southside Serpents, the meanest motorcycle gang in Riverdale. Looking for a fight with anyone who looked at him wrong, Fangs zeroed in on the Riverdale kids, which brought the wrath of Betty and Veronica's Vixens to the Serpents' doorstep. The Vixens beat Fangs at his own race, forcing his gang out of town, and his girlfriend Penny dropped him like an 8-ball in the corner pocket.

SUE STRINGLY

First Appearance:
The Adventures of Little Archie #30, Spring 1964

Sue Stringly lived in a shack near the Riverdale railway
tracks with her family. Despite being poor, Sue was
always upbeat and cheerful and never complained
about her situation. In fact, she would go out of her way to help others.

Sue popped back to Riverdale as a teen secret agent (Agent S) to help
Agents B and V save Archie from the clutches of Evelyn Evernever, who had
trapped him on the Ferris Wheel. No one really knows what she was up to
while she left Riverdale between elementary and high school, but she did
learn a very specific set of skills.

In *Vixens*, Sue joined up with The Thrashers, a rival motorcycle gang to
Betty and Veronica's Vixens. Sue was captured by Mad Doc Doom, but was
rescued by her gang (with a little help from the Vixens).

PENNY PEABODY

First Appearance:
The Adventures of Little Archie #40, Fall 1966

Penny Peabody was Fangs Fogarty's childhood
girlfriend, and was a ray of sunshine compared to
Fangs' grey cloud. Penny always sees the good in
people (including Fangs!) and helps out wherever she can. She's not usually
aware of just how much Fangs defends her, which sometimes leads to a trail
of destruction.

In *Vixens*, as Fangs Fogarty's girlfriend, Penny is one of the few girls allowed
in the Southside Serpents' inner circle. The members of the gang didn't see
her as an equal, though, which didn't work so well for them. After the Vixens
ran the Serpents out of town, Penny and her old friend Bubbles McBounce
turned the old gang home base, Spotty's, into The Perilous Pike, an all-
inclusive bar and hangout.

FORSYTHIA "JELLYBEAN" JONES

First Appearance: *Archie's Pal Jughead Comics* #50, November 1993

Forsythia "Jellybean" Jones is Jughead's baby sister and his biggest fan. She got her nickname because she was born in a traffic jam that was caused by an overturned jellybean truck. She has her own unique style and is very smart, especially when it comes to wrapping Jughead around her finger. She's not so sure about Veronica or Reggie, but loves when Betty comes over to babysit. As a teen, Jellybean worked for her brother at the Chocklit Shoppe, which almost ended in disaster when her no-good boyfriend, Davey, tried to rob it. Jellybean knew something was wrong and tipped Jughead and the authorities off since no matter what, family comes first. She also had the unfortunate luck of inheriting her big bro's werewolf genes!

SOUPHEAD

First Appearance:
Archie Comics #4,
September-October
1943

Souphead Jones is Jughead's younger cousin but might as well be his (smaller!) twin. The cousins also share a love for napping and eating everything in sight, though Souphead prefers (you guessed it) soup to Jughead's burger obsession. Souphead idolizes his older cousin and bugs him at times, but the two have a good relationship. When he's not following Jughead around, Souphead gets into trouble with Leroy Lodge.

LEROY LODGE

First Appearance:
Archie's Joke Book Magazine #31,
November 1957

Leroy Lodge is Veronica's younger cousin and is a bit of a prankster. He's friendly with Souphead Jones and when they're both in town visiting their cousins, the two boys always have some money-making scheme. Leroy loves skateboarding and even raced Archie in his car one time. He's also great at driving R/C cars!

DENISE KELLER

First Appearance:
Veronica #209,
December 2011

Denise Keller is
Kevin's younger
sister. She was born in France while
Col. Keller was away serving so
Kevin stepped up as older brother
and man of the house. The siblings
have a close relationship and Denise
will defend Kevin to the ends of the
earth. Though she is the middle
child, Denise loves being social and
is outspoken at family dinners. She
loves new technology and is rarely
without her tablet.

PATTY KELLER

First Appearance:
Veronica #209,
December 2011

Patty Keller is the
baby of the Keller
family and the only child born in the
United States. She's precocious and
has no filter when she's telling Kevin
what she thinks. She looks up to her
older sister Denise and is always
trying to steal her clothes. Patty is
never too far from the action and
always in a good mood. She has no
fear and loves trying new things!

TERESA LOPEZ

First Appearance:
*Betty and Veronica
Spectacular #50,*
November 2001

Teresa Lopez is
Ginger's younger sister and Eliza's
twin. Like her famous chef father
Eduardo, Teresa loves to cook and is
good at it! She experiments with her
cooking, which doesn't always work
out (no one needs a clam chowder
ice pop), but that never gets her
down. Teresa and Eliza drive Ginger
mad with their exuberance, but the
sisters all love each other at the end
of the day!

ELIZA LOPEZ

First Appearance:
*Betty and Veronica
Spectacular #50,*
November 2001

Eliza Lopez is
Ginger's younger sister and Teresa's
twin. While Teresa is following
her father's footsteps, Eliza is her
mother's shadow. She loves animals
of all kinds and will sneak as many
bugs and rescues into the house as
she can. Like her twin, Eliza is a little
hyperactive and loves to raid her
older sister's closet which usually
has Ginger pulling her hair out.

HOT DOG

First Appearance:
Pep #189, January 1966

Hot Dog is the Jones family dog, though his loyalty is really to Jughead. He's a large fluffy dog and though he's a mutt, he looks a lot like a sheepdog with long white hair covering his eyes. Hot Dog is very intelligent and observant of the people around him, and sometimes wonders what the humans are thinking when they get into scrapes, but he keeps his thoughts to himself. Like his owner, Hot Dog loves napping and eating, though he does have an eye for Veronica's purebred pups. He's an incredibly laid-back dog who goes with the flow, but the one thing he can't abide is cats.

VEGAS

First Appearance:
Archie Jumbo Comics Double Digest #244, November 2013

Vegas is Archie's dog and a very good boy. Betty rescued him from a shelter and gave him to Archie, who happily took him in. Vegas is a caramel-colored, shaggy mutt and is super friendly—he even gets along with Betty's cat! He loves his family and has rescued swimmers when Archie works as a lifeguard at the beach. Vegas has a sophisticated palate and learned from Veronica's poodles how to get the good stuff from the chef when he and Archie are over at the Lodge estate.

SPOTTY

First Appearance:
Little Archie #2, Winter 1956-1957

Spotty was Archie's childhood dog and an honorary member of the gang. He was a brown mutt with black spots and would follow Archie anywhere, even to school! He would chase anything and everything (especially cats) which often led to destruction and chaos. Even though Spotty was a little wild, he also helped Archie and his friends out and tracked other missing pets when they were in trouble.

First Appearance: *Archie Jumbo Comics Double Digest* #244, November 2013

Reggie Mantle adopted Runty from the shelter to use as a girl magnet. Runty definitely attracted girls, but also was a magnet for trouble! Reggie initially intended to return Runty to the shelter, but realized that Runty had quickly found a place in the family and Reggie's heart. When he's not being dognapped, Runty enjoys napping on Reggie's bed and hanging out with the other Riverdale pets (like Hot Dog and Caramel the cat).

CARAMEL

First Appearance:
Little Archie #1, 1956 (as Kitty) / *Little Archie* #2, Winter 1956-1957

Caramel is Betty Cooper's childhood and longtime pet cat. Caramel is intelligent (as cats are) and patient with her owner, but she'll run and hide when she needs to! She can often be found up in a tree, staying safe from the neighborhood dogs (especially Spotty), but also pals around with Vegas, Runty, and Hot Dog. Always curious, Caramel has been known to accidentally hitch a ride in a delivery truck, but she always eventually makes her way back to the Coopers'.

FIFI

First Appearance:
Archie's Girls Betty and Veronica #3 (September 1951)

Fifi is one of Veronica's numerous poodles and is never seen without a bow on her head. She's a purebred pedigree poodle who sometimes sports a lion cut so she can stand out from the pack. Veronica gives her only the best, which includes a full-sized dog house in Veronica's bedroom. Fifi enjoys the finer things in life like French cuisine, but also enjoys running around the park with the other Riverdale pets, especially Hot Dog.

WELCOME TO GREENDALE!

When there's something weird or spooky going on in Riverdale, you can bet Sabrina and her aunts are somewhere to be found. Greendale neighbors Riverdale and has its own meddlesome kids, as well as a few magical animals, Warlocks, and Witches. You can visit, but just be nice or you may find yourself turned into a toad!

SABRINA SPELLMAN

First Appearance:
Archie's Madhouse #22, October 1962

Hair: Light Blonde

Eyes: Blue

Hobbies: Hanging out with friends, spellcasting

Likes: Harvey, her family, her mortal friends

Dislikes: Enchantra, Amber

Sabrina Spellman lives in Greendale and is half-mortal (thanks, mom!) and half-witch (thanks, dad!). She lives with her aunts Hilda and Zelda and Salem the cat, who acts as her familiar. Greendale is the next town over from Riverdale but while Sabrina occasionally hangs out with Archie, Betty, Veronica and the group, she also has her own friends locally and her long-time boyfriend, Harvey. Because Sabrina lives in the mortal world and goes to a normal high school, she has to hide her magical abilities, which isn't always easy! She just wants to help people, but since she's still learning how to be a witch, her spells sometimes (often) backfire. She has her aunts and Salem to help guide her through being a teenage witch, which probably helps Greendale and Riverdale stay on the map. Aside from having the ability to turn her teachers into kids, Sabrina tries to live as a "regular" mortal teen— hanging out with her friends at the soda shoppe, auditioning for the school's talent show, and talking to her cat (except in Sabrina's world, the cat talks back). And while she spends plenty of time at the beach, Sabrina tries to stay out of the water so no one else notices that she won't sink!

DID YOU KNOW?

-Sabrina had her own animated series on CBS that ran from 1971 - 1974. In this version, Sabrina was created by Hilda and Zelda due to a miscast spell (her standard origin story is that she was born of a mortal mother and warlock father).
- Sabrina started the Zombie Apocalypse in Riverdale (whoops!) when she resurrected Jughead's dog (who came back undead and bit Jughead, turning him)

LITTLE SABRINA

Sabrina Spellman was young once! As a child, Sabrina had to keep her magical powers in check while she joined Little Archie and the gang in their elementary school adventures. Her magic usually backfires, but her aunts Hilda and Zelda are there to help clean up the mystical mishaps.

Sabrina at GRAVESTONE HEIGHTS

For a spell (ha!), Sabrina and her aunts moved back to her aunts' old town, Gravestone Heights. It's a town where werewolves, vampires, and witches can all live out in the open without fear of mortals finding them out! Sabrina settles in quickly and dates Drac, a young vampire, and becomes fast friends with Cleara, an invisible girl. Jerome (a male medusa), Milton (a mummy), and Eyeda (a cyclops) round out Sabrina's friend group.

In *Sabrina: The Animated Series*, Sabrina is a tween attending Greendale Middle School. Her best friend, Chloe Flan, is a mortal who knows Sabrina's secret. Classmate Gemini "Gem" Stone is the rich, popular girl in school and Sabrina's main rival who also has a crush on Harvey, Sabrina's good friend (who she *also* has a crush on). Tween Sabrina is still trying to figure out how to use her magic and sometimes causes chaos in the school or around town. She has Salem to help guide her as well as her aunts, Hilda and Zelda, who she lives with, but even their good advice can't stop her and Chloe from getting into trouble.

When Sabrina's friend Llandra wanted to know more about the art style of Manga, the two girls transported into a whole Manga-style world! In this version of Sabrina, inspired by Shuojo and Magical Girl Manga, Sabrina splits her time between Baxter High School and her mortal friends and Spellcasting School and her new group of magical friends. Things get a little complicated when she tries to keep the two worlds separated so that her mortal crush, Harvey, and her magical crush, Shinji, don't overlap!

CHILLING ADVENTURES OF SABRINA

Sabrina was taken from her mortal mother when she was just a year old and given to her aunts Hilda and Zelda to be raised. Her aunts teach her how to use her powers and her familiar, Salem (a cat), helps be her moral guide, but Sabrina still has to figure out how to blend in as a mortal teen cheerleader during her daytimes at Baxter High School while learning the dark arts and her even darker history at home.

On her 16th birthday, Sabrina needs to decide if she wants to be baptized into the Church of Nigh or lose all of her powers and live out her life as a mortal.

In the *Chilling Adventures of Sabrina* Netflix series, the town of Greendale is a darker telling of Sabrina's story. She and her aunts live in an old manse with Salem, Sabrina's cat (and familiar), and Ambrose, her cousin who has been kicked out of boarding school for revealing his powers to mortals. Sabrina was taken from her mother, Diana, as a baby with her father Edward's blessing and given to his sisters, Hilda and Zelda, to raise. As a half-mortal, half-witch, Sabrina attends Baxter High School with the mortals and dates star football player Harvey Kinkle, who has no idea that she's part witch. On her 16th birthday, Sabrina must decide whether to give up her powers and live as a mortal or be baptized into the Church of Night. Not everyone will make it out of Greendale's woods alive.

HILDA SPELLMAN

First Appearance:
Archie's Madhouse #24, February 1963

Hilda Spellman is Sabrina's paternal aunt and sister to Zelda Spellman. She's tall and skinny and has a sharp nose and a prominent mole on her chin. If you ask Hilda, she's beautiful and Sabrina is the one who could use a makeover. Hilda is anywhere from 300 to 700 years old (one never asks a witch her age) and dresses like it with her long black robes and pointed hat. She's strict with Sabrina, but it's just because she wants her to be the best witch she can be. In later iterations, Hilda developed a great sense of style and is highly skilled at spellcasting.

ZELDA SPELLMAN

First Appearance:
Archie's Madhouse #65, December 1968

Zelda Spellman is Sabrina's paternal aunt and Hilda's sister. Where Hilda is tall and thin, Zelda is equally short and round. Even though she's over 300 years old and dresses in puritanical robes and a pointy hat, Zelda sports a bright green bob. She's much friendlier than her sister and helps Sabrina with her spells as well as giving her guidance on living in the mortal realm. In later iterations, Zelda is a bit of a wild child with short, spiky green hair. In the Middle Ages, Zelda was engaged to the popular minstrel, Metal Melborne. She broke off the engagement, but he popped up again in modern times as a rock star who tried to win Zelda back (and failed).

SALEM SABERHAGEN

First Appearance:
Archie's Madhouse #22, October 1962

Salem Saberhagen was a warlock, but is
currently an American Shorthair cat who
acts as Sabrina's familiar. There have been
many reasons behind his punishment to
live life out as a cat. In one, Salem was a
warlock bent on world domination. In another, he was turned into a cat as
punishment for leaving Head Witch Enchantra at the altar. In the Chilling
Sabrina universe, Salem (nee Samuel), was a human who landed in Boston in
1692 and labored on a local's farm where he met Abigail, a maid who was also
a witch. He got her pregnant and when he refused to marry Abigail, she cursed
him and transformed him into a cat as punishment. As Sabrina's familiar
and confidante, Salem can speak and is fluent in sarcasm. Despite his surly
attitude, he cares for Sabrina and helps her figure out how to perform spells
and navigate life as a witch in the mortal realm.

HARVEY KINKLE

First Appearance:
Archie's T.V. Laugh-Out #1, December 1969

Harvey Kinkle is a student at Baxter High
School and Sabrina's boyfriend. Though
they're dating, he's mortal and is blissfully
unaware that Sabrina is a witch. Harvey is
a nerdy and very klutzy, but he's loyal to
Sabrina. In Chilling Sabrina, Harvey is Sabrina's boyfriend and a star football
player. Harvey didn't know that Sabrina and her aunts were witches until
Madam Satan set him up to stumble upon Sabrina's baptism in the woods.
He attempted to escape from the coven's wrath but was tricked by Madam
Satan who killed him with her kiss. His body was used as a vessel to resurrect
Edward, Sabrina's Father and Madam Satan's former lover.

AMBROSE PIPPS

First Appearance:
Archie's T.V. Laugh-Out #1, December 1969

Ambrose is Sabrina's cousin, a talented warlock
who's over 800 years old. He's well-dressed
and has a dry sense of humor. Ambrose plays
interference between Sabrina and her Aunt Hilda when they clash. He's been
known to accidentally let the family's secret out or perform experiments that
don't end quite as they should.

In *Chilling Sabrina*, Ambrose is Sabrina's impulsive cousin who moved in
with Hilda, Zelda, and Sabrina with his familiars, cobras Nag and Nagaina.
Ambrose was sent to the Spellmans because he reveluted his magic by taking
someone's hands which led to him being kicked out of his boarding school.

UNCLE QUIGGLY

First Appearance:
Sabrina #1, (2000 Series) January 2000

Quigley is Sabrina's maternal great-uncle and adult
guardian to Sabrina. He's a portly mortal and tries to
keep order and sanity in the house. Though he seems unreasonable at times,
he deep down just wants to keep Sabrina and her aunts safe.

ENCHANTRA

First Appearance:
Sabrina the Teenage Witch #15, June 1998

Enchantra is the Queen of Witches and head of
the Witches' Council. She disdains mortals and if
anyone wrongs Enchantra (in reality or imagined),
they had better be able to run fast and hide! She and Salem (yes, that Salem)
were engaged at one point but when he called off the wedding, Enchantra
turned him into a cat. Cousin Ambrose was also engaged to Enchantra, but
realized his error and broke off the engagement with Salem's help.

MADAM SATAN

First Appearance:
Pep Comics #16, June 1941

Madam Iola Satan was a mortal who killed her fiancé's parents because they didn't approve of the marriage. Before they died, they told their son and he, in turn, killed Iola. She went to hell where she became Satan's partner. Satan sent her back to earth to seduce men and kill them, sending their souls to hell. While she outwardly is beautiful, Madam Satan's real face is a skull and her kiss will kill men. In *Chilling Sabrina*, Iola was Edward Spellman's former love and the woman he left for Diana, Sabrina's mother. Edward wanted a child, which Madam Satan, as a witch, couldn't give him. Because of Edward's betrayal, Madam Satan threw herself into the lion pit at the zoo where her body was devoured and her soul went to Gehenna, the capitol city of Hell. She was then conjured from a forest lake by Betty and Veronica, who were attempting magic without knowing what they were about to release. A faceless Madam Satan rose from the depths of hell, stole a woman's face, and started to exact her revenge on the Spellmans. In order to get closer to Sabrina and plan her revenge, Madam Satan uses her new identity as Evangeline Porter to fill in for the drama teacher at Baxter High School. Eventually Madam Satan kills Harvey and resurrects Edward in his body.

DELLA

First Appearance:
Archie's Madhouse #22, October 1962

Della was the Spellmans' Head Witch and assigned Sabrina to hex the students at Baxter High School. She tried to get Sabrina to be a proper witch, but was usually frustrated that Sabrina wasn't devious and would use her magic to help mortals instead of cause chaos. In later years, Della is the no-nonsense personal assistant to Head Witch Enchantra. She's always buttoned-up and wears her hair in a tight bun—Satan-forbid that she ever have a little fun in her life! She helps Enchantra keep the Spellmans in check for the Witches' Council and helps keep Enchantra's anger in check.

AMBER NIGHTSTONE

First Appearance: *Sabrina Anniversary Spectacular* #1, September 2022

Hair: Fiery Red

Eyes: Red

Hobbies: Casting hexes, playing with fire, schemeing to enter the mortal realm

Likes: Snakes, concocting potions, spicy foods

Dislikes: Sabrina

Watch out, Sabrina—a new nemesis has made her way to Greendale! And unlike the teens Sabrina has faced off against before, this one has an edge: she's also a witch! Amber Nightstone is an evil witch born exactly at the same time and on the same day as Sabrina. Per the Code of Sorcery, only one witch born that day may live among mortals—and Amber wants her turn, which means that she must erase Sabrina from history on her seventeenth birthday!

With her signature bright red and yellow hair resembling flames, fiery is an apt word to describe Amber's personality! Like Sabrina, Amber also has a familiar, a pet snake named Percy. The duo proved to be formidable opponents for Sabrina and Salem, until head witch Della stepped in and returned order, trapping Amber in an hourglass. But a teen witch with as much personality and power as Amber can't be held back for long!

COUSIN ESMERALDA

First Appearance:
Sabrina the Teenage Witch #67, June 1981

Esmeralda is Sabrina's younger cousin who comes to visit from time to time. She's in the Junior Witches League (the witch version of Girl Scouts) and can be an obnoxious brat at times and often uses her magic without thinking. Esmeralda doesn't always appreciate that Sabrina might know best, but as they spend more time together, Esmeralda grew to respect her cousin and look up to her.

ROZ

First Appearance:
Chilling Adventures of Sabrina #1
December 2014

Rosalind (or Roz or Rossy, depending on how much she likes you) is a classmate of Sabrina's at Baxter High School. She's a popular girl and has made competing with Sabrina her mission. To stack the odds, Roz will spread rumors and gossip about Sabrina and used to date Harvey before Sabrina came into the picture. Roz has no shame in hooking up with Harvey (really Edward, resurrected) when he comes back to school after his disappearance even though he's presumably still with Sabrina.

GEM STONE

First Appearance:
Sabrina #1,
January 2000

Gemini "Gem" Stone is Sabrina's snobby, pampered classmate at Greendale Middle School. Her family is the richest in town and Gem will never let anyone forget that! Gem loves fashion and wouldn't be caught wearing the same outfit twice (sometimes that's because a spell from Sabrina has ruined her clothing). Gem is a dancer and competes with Sabrina for everything, especially Harvey's affections. Gem might be the most popular girl at school and the richest girl around, but she still can't steal Harvey's eye away from Sabrina for long!

SHINJI YAGAMI

First Appearance:
Sabrina the Teenage Witch #40, February 2003

Shinji Yamagi is Sabrina's handsome spellcasting classmate. He's a great warlock-in-training, but lives with Spellexia so watch out in case he accidentally summons a Greek god instead of a furry dog! Shinji has a crush on Sabrina (the feeling is mutual), but knows she's loyal to Harvey. He does manage to get her to play his favorite game, Magic Monsters, an RPG that the magic realm kids play for real, leaving the table-top version to the mortals.

BRUCE VAN KLOOD

First Appearance:
Archie's Madhouse #28, September 1963

Bruce Van Klood is an upper crust Baxter High School student who enjoys the finer things like playing tennis at the club. He's handsome enough to catch Sabrina's eye, but dim enough that he picks her rival, Rosalind, as his doubles partner (for tennis AND the soda shoppe!).

AMY REINHARDT

First Appearance:
Sabrina the Teenage Witch #3, July 1997

Amy Reinhardt is one of the popular girls at Baxter High School and competes with Sabrina for anything she can. She has the occasional lapse and can be nice, but always pulls that in to maintain her mean girl attitude. It doesn't help that Amy has a crush on Harvey, so she enjoys being extra to try and pull his eyes away from Sabrina. (Spoiler alert: he only has eyes for Sabrina.)

LIANDRA DA SILVA

First Appearance:
Sabrina #9, September 2000

Llandra da Silva and Sabrina met when they both attended Camp Nethernether Land. The girls became fast friends as they shared the experience of being witches living in the mortal realm. Llandra's father is a famous South American Jungle Shaman and she carries the tradition with her "green powers" (meaning she can travel via root system and make magic with plants!).

QUEEN SELES

First Appearance: *Sabrina the Teenage Witch #60*, October 2004

The Elven Queen Seles, Czarina of Balance is the leader of the High Council and the most powerful sorceress in the Magic Realm. It is her job as queen to protect the Mana Tree, the source of all magic energy throughout the realm. When Vosblanc absorbs Seles' magic with a soulstone she loses all magical abilities, and the Mana tree begins to die. She keeps this a secret from the realm, except for her trusted guards who form the Four Blades in order to protect the queen.

NARAYAN

First Appearance: *Sabrina the Teenage Witch #77*, September 2006

Narayan is a Merman from the underwater city of Melusina, where any form of art besides architecture is outlawed. When Narayan discovers the ancient cave paintings of his ancestors, he is inspired to tell stories through his own paintings. When he realizes that his ancestors' prophecies are about the Mana tree dying, he joins Shinji, Sabrina, and Llandra as the fourth member of the revival of the Four Blades. After falling in love with Llandra, Sabrina creates a spell that allows him to walk on land whenever he emerges from the water.

GRETA

First Appearance: *Archie's Madhouse #28*, September 1963

Greta is Sabrina's "Fairy Witch Mother" who acts as a mentor to Sabrina. She often appears, without warning, to encourage Sabrina to use her powers in difficult situations.

CHLOE

First Appearance: *Sabrina the Teenage Witch #32*, December 1999

Chloe Flan is Sabrina's best friend at Greendale Middle School. She is one of the only mortals that knows Sabrina is a witch, as she is often involved in her magical hijinks.

CLEARA

First Appearance:
Archie & Friends #2,
November 1992

The invisible Cleara Glass
is the first friend Sabrina
makes when she moves to
Gravestone Heights. Cleara
embraces herself with
makeup, accessories, and
her signature hair bow. She
is often seen in an "Invisible
and Proud" tee shirt.

EYEDA

First Appearance:
Archie & Friends #6,
October 1993

Eyeda is another one of
Sabrina's close friends
at Gravestone Heights.
She always keeps her
hair pulled back in a
ponytail, to keep her
hair out of her eye.

CHIP

First Appearance:
Archie & Friends #2,
November 1992

Chip Noggin is a
fellow student at
Gravestone Heights.
He is the great
grandson of the
original headless
horseman and can
completely remove his
head from his body!

MS. REAPER

First Appearance:
Archie & Friends #5,
August 1993

Ms. Reaper is a teacher
at Gravestone Heights.
Her face is covered by
the hood of the cloak
that she wears, but
underneath she's really a
skeleton. Her hex exams
are hard, so you'd better
study! You don't want to
get ex-spelled!

WELCOME TO JOSIE AND THE PUSSYCATS!

Josie and the Pussycats might be the most accomplished band in comic book history! Josie, Valerie, and Melody started as an average girl group, with dreams of making it big. It wasn't until they branded themselves "Josie and The Pussycats," that they really made a name for themselves, becoming the most popular band in Midvale, Riverdale, and eventually the world! Their friendship is responsible for the group's success, as their chemistry is apparent both onstage and off.

Their chart-topping hits include the songs "Stop, Look & Listen," "You've Come a Long Way Baby," "3 Small Words," "Pretend to Be Nice," and of course "Josie and the Pussycats." Each girl brings something different to the group dynamic. Josie is the driving force behind the band, Valerie is the brain behind the music, and Melody is the heart.

JOSIE MCCOY

First Appearance: *Archie's Pals 'n' Gals* #23, 1963

Hair: Red

Eyes: Blue/Green

Hobbies: Playing guitar and singing, tennis, hiking, roller blading

Likes: Rock 'n' Roll, Performing, Dancing, Exercising/Fitness, sewing, upcycling clothes from the thrift store, Alan M.

Dislikes: Mishaps on stage, when things are out of her control, giving up, being unprepared

DID YOU KNOW?

-Legendary Archie artist Dan DeCarlo, who created Josie and friends, named Josie after his wife.

-The Pussycats original costumes were made by Josie herself! Who knew she was so good at sewing?

-Josie's original last name was Jones! It wasn't changed to McCoy until the release of the *Josie and the Pussycats* movie in 2001! Maybe she's related to Jughead Jones?

-Josie has an extensive collection of rock and roll vinyl records. She hopes the Pussycats release one of their albums on vinyl someday!

Josie McCoy is the lead vocalist and guitarist for Josie and the Pussycats, and is all about Rock 'n' Roll! Josie is known for her great initiative, especially when it comes to the career of the Pussycats, as she always puts the band first, and does everything she can to help them succeed. Before the band hit it big, they rehearsed in Josie's garage after school. Josie would make merch to sell at their small shows in Riverdale, anything to get their name out there! Josie's boyfriend Alan M. is the Pussycat's roadie, but she never lets her feelings for him get in the way of the band. Josie may be busy touring the world with The Pussycats, but always does her best to maintain her friendships back home.

While Josie McCoy is now known for her musical abilities, she was not originally introduced as a Pussycat. After appearing in *Archie's Pals 'n' Gals*, Josie was given her own comic in 1963. The series ran as *She's Josie* and followed Josie and Melody in high school, before they met Valerie and formed Josie and the Pussycats. *She's Josie* included the first iteration of several characters who are now staple cast members of Josie's world including Alexander Cabot III and his sister Alexandra, whose family's wealth often funded their misadventures. There were also characters who would eventually step back from the comics after the rebranding, such as Pepper and her boyfriend Sock, as well as Josie's first boyfriend Albert. Albert and Alexander fought often for Josie's affections, which would only lead her closer to Pepper and Melody.

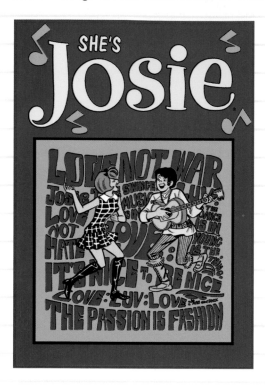

"Josie and the Pussycats, long tails and ears for hats!" In 1970, The Pussycats went on tour! Joined by the Cabot siblings and Alan M., the gang found themselves mixed up in all sorts of trouble all over the world in the *Josie and the Pussycats* cartoon from Hanna-Barbera. It was the development of this series that led the *She's Josie* comics into being retooled from high school stories, to the *Josie and the Pussycats* musical adventures with issue 45, introducing Valerie Smith into the cast.

In 1972 The Pussycats traded in their cat ears for spacesuits in *Josie and the Pussycats in Outer Space*. The series was filled with just as many bizarre adventures as the first one, but this time the characters were joined by a fluffy alien named "Bleep" as they travelled across the Milky Way. This series made its debut in comics as a sci-fi horror digital comic in 2019.

In 2005 The Pussycats were also given the manga treatment. After bonding over their love for rock music, Josie Jones and Valerie Smith form Josie and the Pussycats, with Melody Valentine, whose idea it is to wear their cat outfits, although her own costume is often pink and frillier. The girls are often reviewed on their fashion rather than their music, so they experiment with different styles as they play miscellaneous shows around Midvale.

In the CW *Riverdale* series, Josephine "Josie" McCoy is played by Ashleigh Murray. It was Josie's idea to form Josie and the Pussycats after meeting Valerie and Melody when they all worked together at Power Records. Josie is a natural leader who, as lead singer and guitarist, makes the Pussycats her number one priority at all times. She receives a lot of pressure to succeed in music from her mother, who describes Josie's talents as irreplaceable. Mayor McCoy might be very strict with her daughter but she still supports her in all her Pussycat endeavours, unlike Josie's father, who sees the Pussycats as childish.

This has led Josie to seek her father's approval more than anyone else's. Josie works hard to try to push her band to super stardom and gets frustrated when her bandmates don't take rehearsals as seriously as she believes they should. This has led to many different variations of the Pussycats throughout her time in Riverdale. Although she can be pushy and often takes her emotions out on other people, Josie really is a caring person at heart who goes to great lengths for her friends. Josie also appeared in the *Riverdale* spin off series *Katy Keene* where she moved to New York after high school.

VALERIE SMITH

First Appearance: *Josie and the Pussycats* #45, 1969

Hair: Brunette

Eyes: Brown

Hobbies: Playing the bass, writing, journaling, planning (she keeps a very detailed planner, someone has to keep track of all The Pussycat's gigs!)

Likes: Song writing, pizza, travelling/sightseeing, jam sessions, studying, reading, babysitting, documentaries, puzzles

Dislikes: Attention, paparazzi, disorganization

Valerie is the bassist for the Pussycats, but she can also play guitar and the tambourine. Although she usually only provides backup vocals, Val has a great voice and has taken the lead on several occasions. Valerie is the most level-headed of the Pussycats, and is an extremely loyal friend. She's not afraid to stand up to people, as she's the first person to put the Cabots in their place when their selfish actions affect the band. Valerie likes to focus on the present and enjoy life right in front of her. She is also smart and has an extensive knowledge of musical instruments and their history. She always tries to research wherever the Pussycats are travelling to so she can appreciate the experience even more.

DID YOU KNOW?
-On a temporary break from the band, Valerie used her talents to sell custom designed bass guitars!
-Val isn't just a songwriter for The Pussycats, she's also helped other performers with their lyrics, writing songs for The Archies, The Bingoes, The Madhouse Glads, Brigitte Reilly, and Frankie Valdez.
-When the Pussycats aren't on tour, Valerie picks up jobs babysitting, tutoring, and teaching kids music. Talk about a cool role model!

The Archies and Josie and the Pussycats cross paths quite often, but it wasn't until the two bands went on tour in 2010 (*Archie* #608), that Archie and Valerie spend real one-on-one time together. They connect over pizza while writing the song "More Than Words" and fall head over heels for each other. They agree to keep their relationship a secret until the end of the tour, but their chemistry is obvious to not only their friends, but the audience as well. The lovebirds are separated when The Pussycats tour Europe but reconnect despite Alexander's attempts to split them up.

In "Another Love Song" (*Archie* #631, 2012) the Smith family moves to Riverdale and Archie and Valerie continue their relationship right where they left off. (We even get a glimpse into their future together when Valerie walks up Riverdale's infamous Memory Lane). Veronica is surprised how composed Betty is about Archie dating Valerie, until it is discovered that Betty and Trev (Valerie's brother) have been dating in secret! This leads to an argument between Archie and Valerie because of how protective Archie is over Betty. But their love for each other is so strong that this argument doesn't last very long.

Their relationship is often considered "off again on again," as they both try to put their friendships first, and do what's best for both bands. In fact, when the bands tour together for a second time, Archie and Valerie snub each other, to avoid any potential jealousy from their bandmates. Valerie affectionately calls Archie "Red."

MELODY VALENTINE

First Appearance: *Archie's Pals 'n' Gals* #23, 1963

Hair: Blonde

Eyes: Blue

Hobbies: Playing the drums, volunteering at the animal shelter

Likes: Spending time with her friends, percussion, kittens, puppies, pink, fashion, plushies, coloring

Dislikes: Nothing! Well maybe bullies, or party poopers!

Melody marches to the beat of her own drum! Maybe that's why she's the drummer for Josie and the Pussycats! Melody is often pursued by men because of her looks, but she's got a lot more going for her! She's the most caring person you'll ever meet, and is very passionate about the things she enjoys. She might not be the brightest, but don't underestimate her! She just has a different perspective on life. Melody might be a little too trusting at times, but she always has Josie and Valerie with her to watch her back.

DID YOU KNOW?

-Melody may be the Pussycats drummer, but she is almost always singing! She is known for embellishing her sentences with music notes.

-Melody loves all animals, especially kittens! She volunteers often at animal shelters, and would take all the animals home if she could!

-Melody loves hosting parties! If she finds out it's someone's birthday, she'll throw a surprise party for sure! (But she'll probably let it slip ahead of time. Oops!)

TREVOR SMITH

First Appearance:
Archie #631, March 28, 2012

Trevor "Trev" Smith is the younger brother of Josie and the Pussycats star Valerie Smith, and is a talented musician just like his sister. He can play guitar and can even sing a little too. Trev believes that music tells a story, with or without lyrics, and wants to be a film score composer. He is a big movie buff, and specifically loves horror movies because of the dramatic music. When Trev and his family move to Riverdale, he attends Riverdale High School, and starts spending more time with the Archie gang. Trev and Betty kick it off right away and soon start dating.

DID YOU KNOW?

-Trev loves watching silent movies. The lack of dialogue really lets the emotion in the music speak for itself.
-Trev keeps a journal and often flips back through it when he needs some inspiration.
-When the Pussycats travel to New York, Trev always tags along in hopes of seeing a Broadway show or two. He just loves the combination of storytelling and music!

First Appearance:
She's Josie #1, February 1963

The Cabot twins are always up to no good, and The Pussycats are always caught right in the middle of it. As the Pussycats' manager, Alexander Cabot III is in charge of all the band's endeavors, but his sister Alexandra always interrupts his plans in an attempt to steal the spotlight. Not only does Alexandra want Josie's position as lead pussycat, but she's constantly trying to win over her boyfriend as well! The Cabot twins often work together to break the couple up, since Alex has a thing for Josie. The siblings come from a wealthy family, which is how they can afford their lavish schemes.

DID YOU KNOW?

-Alexandra has magical powers! It is unclear if she is a witch or not, but some say her powers come from her cat Sebastian, others say it's from the white streak in her hair. (Sabrina also has white hair but maybe that's just a coincidence. I wonder if Salem and Sebastian know each other…)
-After becoming the Pussycats manager, Alexander is almost always seen with his signature sunglasses, even indoors! He thinks it will help him be taken more seriously, but Alexandra begs to differ.

PEPPER SMITH

First Appearance:
Archie's Pals 'n' Gals #23, December 1962

Pepper Smith is Josie and Melody's best friend from high school. She is especially close to Josie, as the two grew up together. Pepper is often skeptical of others, but that might be from spending too much time with the Cabots! Pepper likes to dress up just as much as her friends, and is usually seen sporting a preppy look with her signature "cat eye" glasses. Sometimes she can be a little temperamental, but that's just because she cares about her friends, and is very aware of how the boys in school treat them. She just wants to make sure that her friends are protected from any unwanted attention. Pepper loves being outdoors, and is often seen walking around town with her boyfriend Sock. The two girls may have moved away from each other, but don't worry! Josie and Pepper still maintain a close friendship and get together whenever The Pussycats are in town!

ALAN M. MAYBERRY

First Appearance: *Josie* #42, August 1969

Alan M. Mayberry is Josie and the Pussycats' roadie. He is the muscle of the group, and would do anything to protect his girlfriend, Josie. He is very loyal to the band, and tries to do everything himself, reluctant to ask anyone for help. Alan's intelligence is often compared to Melody's, but maybe that's why Josie loves him so much, because he reminds her of one of her best friends.

ALBERT

First Appearance:
She's Josie #1,
February 1963

Albert is Josie's high school sweetheart and first boyfriend. He is a musician and is often seen with his acoustic guitar. He comes up with his own music, but often has a hard time rhyming his lyrics. Unless he's with Josie, who he considers his muse, even stating "everything I sing is inspired by Josie." Maybe because Albert was so passionate about his daughter, Josie's father was not very fond of him and referred to him as a hippie!

SOCK

Socrates, or Sock as he is known by his peers, is Pepper's boyfriend and Albert's best friend. Sock can come off as intimidating because of his tall stature and broad physique, but he is actually a very likable guy, who would do anything for his girlfriend.

WELCOME TO KATY KEENE!

Katy Keene is truly the pinup queen, taking the fashion world by storm since the '40s! Katy has tried it all, but she is best known for her career as a model and actress. After her parents passed away when she was in college, Katy became the legal guardian of her little sister MacKenzie (Sis), who means the world to her. Katy has always been close with her fans, and they just won't let her retire! They support Katy with fan magazines, T-shirts, buttons, and—most notably—fashion designs! Katy had always been interested in sewing, and learned how when she was in high school, but took a break from making her own outfits when she started in college. After she started modeling, Katy's fans started to send her ideas of what they thought she should wear, and Katy took the drawings and made the clothes herself. (Don't worry, Katy always gives credit to her fans!) Soon her fans even started designing looks for her friends, boyfriends, and even Sis! Katy loves providing fans with paper doll versions of her outfits, which they can cut out, and collect. While the spotlight is often overwhelming, Katy uses it as an opportunity to be a role model.

KATY KEENE

First Appearance:
Wilbur Comics #5, June 1945
Hair: Brunette
Eyes: Blue
Hobbies: Modeling, acting, singing, ice skating, snowboarding, tennis, sewing,
Likes: Clothing, dressing up, Avant Garde fashion, attending events/parties, taking care of her little sister
Dislikes: Shallow celebrities, being overworked, not getting to spend enough time with her friends and family, best dressed and worst dressed lists, (just let people wear what they want to wear!)

Katy grew up in the smalltown of Stemville, Michigan, which is most likely why she is so level-headed despite her new Hollywood lifestyle. Katy started her career as a model, and became known for her endearing personality, and natural charm in front of the camera. On set, Katy would quickly make friends with the people she worked with, while still remaining a professional. Once Katy made a name for herself as a model, she took the opportunity to pursue her other interests such as singing and acting. Katy was noticed in Hollywood for her natural talent and good reputation, and was reached out to about small film roles. Katy's big break as an actress was when she starred alongside Topher McWire in *The Web*.

DID YOU KNOW?

-In high school, Katy tried every extracurricular her school offered. She just wanted to do it all!
-Katy is known for having a strong relationship with her fans. She always takes them into consideration before determining her next career move.
-Before finding her passion as a model, Katy was in school studying to become a teacher. Maybe that's what made her such a good guardian for Sis!
-Katy actively avoids rewatching any of her films after they premiere. She just can't get into them, because all she can think about is how much fun she had filming. It ruins the movie magic!

Katy Keene

Katy and friends were brought from the pages to the screen for the first time ever, with the CW show *Katy Keene*. Katherine "Katy" Keene is played by Lucy Hale. Katy is named after her mother, whom she shared her love of fashion with. Katy's mother used the same sewing machine her mother had, which she then passed down to Katy. Katy lives in New York with best friend Jorge Lopez (also known as Ginger Lopez on stage), and her new roommate Josie McCoy (Yes! That Josie McCoy!), who she met through their mutual friend Veronica Lodge (Yes! That Veronica Lodge!). Katy is an aspiring fashion designer, and works at the luxury department store Lacy's, under her boss Gloria Grandbilt.

Katy's ambitious nature was noticed by Gloria, and she was often chosen to assist her personally, although after hearing that Katy designs her own clothing, Gloria warns her that she will need to be more dedicated to Lacy's. Other characters include Katy's boyfriend KO Kelly, New York socialite Pepper Smith, and the Cabot siblings Alexander and Alexandra. (That's a lot of Josie characters!) The show takes place in the same universe as *Riverdale*, of which Katy herself even appeared in an episode!

MACKENZIE (SIS) KEENE

First Appearance: *Wilbur Comics #5*, June, 1945

Affectionately called "Sis" by her older sister Katy, MacKenzie is a fun and creative child, who always keeps herself busy. Sis is astonished by the seemingly lavish lifestyle of her older sister, but Katy always keeps her grounded. While Sis might be intrigued by Katy's world, she prefers to stay out of the spotlight, and tries to spend as much time with her friends as possible. She also values the importance of her education, and is very studious. Although Katy is always there to watch after her, Sis has become very self-sufficient, as she never wants Katy to have to worry about her. Sis loves to bake, and dreams of opening "Sis's Sweets Shop" someday. The two sisters are very close, and Sis remains Katy's biggest fan.

OH THANK YOU, KATY! YOU'RE THE BEST!

DID YOU KNOW?

-Her sister might be the talented Katy Keene, but Sis has her own talents as well. Sis is quite the talented dancer, and started tap classes when she was three! She is also somewhat of an artist, working primarily with acrylic paint.

-Sis has always had quite the sweet tooth. Her parents even nicknamed her "Sis the Candy Kid."

First Appearance: *Wilbur #14*, August 1947

K.O. Kelly is Katy's boyfriend and is a star boxer. K.O. spends most of his free time training, but he and Katy always make time for each other. The couple took a break when they needed to focus more on their careers, but fate ultimately led them back together, as K.O. was the stunt coordinator for her movie The Web He may come across as a tough guy, but K.O. really is a sweetheart, and treats Katy with the respect she deserves.

DID YOU KNOW?

-K.O. has absolutely no spice tolerance and doesn't understand how his girlfriend can enjoy spicy food.
-K.O. doesn't know his own strength! Katy often has to remind him to be gentler, as he has broken quite a few of his belongings by accident, just by picking them up.
-K.O. is incredibly good at hula hooping, and spun his hoop over 10,000 times before losing count! (He says it's good for training, but Katy knows he just thinks it's fun).

GLORIA GOLD

First Appearance:
Pep Comics #94,
November 1952

Although the two
have been friendly at
times, the glamorous Gloria Gold
is Katy's rival, often losing jobs to
Katy because of her off-putting
and vain attitude. She comes from
a wealthy family and is only out
for fame. Gloria's real last name
is "Grandbilt," but she changed it
to "Gold" for her modeling career
because she thought it sounded
more elegant.

KEISHA DUBOIS

First Appearance:
Archie & Friends
#107, April 2007

Keisha DuBois is a
singer and television
personality best known for winning
"America's New Best Model." After
her victory, Keisha returned to
the show to make her live singing
debut, and met Katy who was
guest judging that episode. The
two soon became quick friends,
and even toured together.

RANDY VON RONSON

First Appearance:
Laugh Comics #23,
Summer 1947

Randy Van Ronson
became the world's
wealthiest tycoon before he even
turned thirty. His brief romance
with Katy began after the two
met at her movie premiere (much
to the disapproval of his cousin
Gloria). He's a nice guy, but often
tries to use his wealth to impress
Katy, which fails to work almost
every time.

WELCOME TO JINX!

The Li'l Jinx adventures follow Jinx Holliday and her friends Charley, Greg, Mort, Gigi, Roz, and Russ, as they navigate life as children. Li'l Jinx and friends often tease each other, but all in good fun and nobody's feelings are hurt. They know that when push comes to shove, they have each other's backs. The friends spend most of their time outside together running around the neighborhood, playing games and causing trouble (But nothing too wild!). The kids play baseball and even though they can be competitive, they make a pretty good team. Although there tends to be frequent misunderstandings between the children, they are still close. When she is not out with her friends, Li'l Jinx is often home with her father, who fails to see the importance in Li'l Jinx dilemmas. Although he can get frustrated with his daughter, he knows that she's just a little girl, who has a different understanding of the world than he does.

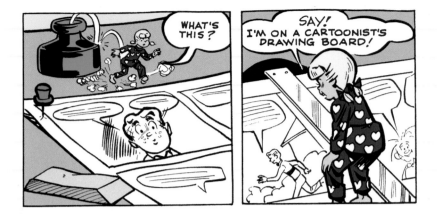

LI'L JINX HOLLIDAY

First Appearance: *Pep Comics* #62, July 1947

Hair: Blonde

Eyes: Green

Hobbies: Baseball, drawing, ice skating, roller skating, fishing

Likes: The color red, watching TV, swimming, puzzles, bananas, ice cream (especially banana splits!), yoyos, dolls, toys, snow, comic books, learning new words, being outdoors

Dislikes: Meatloaf, spinach, rain, cleaning/picking up after herself, being told what to do

Li'l Jinx Holliday is an imaginative little girl, who would rather spend the day outside playing with her friends than doing anything else. Li'l Jinx is easily distracted, and has trouble listening to her father. She often upsets her dad, who becomes frustrated when they have trouble communicating. Despite this, Li'l Jinx is particularly attached to her father because her mother isn't around much. Li'l Jinx is a huge baseball fan, and dreams of playing the sport professionally someday.

DID YOU KNOW?

-Li'l Jinx was born on Halloween! Every year her friends come over for a costume party to celebrate!

-Li'l Jinx is just a nickname! Li'l Jinx hates her real name so much that she won't tell even her closest friends what it is! Only her parents know her real name (and they've been sworn to secrecy!)

-Li'l Jinx is a big Josie and the Pussycats fan! She knows every single one of their songs, and will often perform them loudly throughout the house (much to the dismay of her father.)

-Li'l Jinx and her friends live in the same neighborhood as the Wilkin and Smythe families! They always buy her girl scout cookies!

JINX™

In 2012 Li'l Jinx fans got to see her all grown up for the first time ever in *Jinx*. Starting in the *Life with Archie* magazines, and eventually receiving two graphic novels *Jinx* and *Jinx: Little Miss Steps*, the series follows a 14-year-old Jinx as she starts high school with her childhood friends; Charley, Greg, Mort, Gigi, Roz, and Russ. The series strives to be realistic with the issues Jinx runs into as she's becoming more independent. Life is more complicated for Jinx since she's a pre-teen. Now that she's graduated little league, baseball is for boys, and the girls have to audition for softball. Upset by the lack of sport options for girls, Jinx makes a point to try out for the football team, against both her father and the school's wishes. Jinx isn't about to let anyone tell her what she can and can't do!

Jinx struggles when her mom keeps blowing her off for work, and begins to resent their relationship. And if life wasn't complicated enough, it seems both Greg and Charley have developed a crush on Jinx, and she doesn't understand how to handle this change in their dynamic, let alone her own feelings for either boy!

As a teen, we begin to learn more about the darker side of Jinx's personality. In the *Jughead: the Hunger vs. Vampironica* mini-series, we learned that Jinx's name wasn't just a cute nickname: instead, Jinx was the anti-Christ herself, and she creates chaos in the multiverse thanks to casting a spell she read from the Book of Lucifer.

CHILLING ADVENTURES PRESENTS...

GRIM FAIRY TALES

Jinx's special relationship to books would continue in *Jinx: Grim Fairy Tales*, where we learn that Jinx possesses another unique book: a large tome of fairy tales. But these aren't your typical fables, these are all gruesomely grim stories with herself often playing devil's advocate (if not the devil herself). Jinx likes to read from this book to the unruly children she babysits.

CHARELY HAWSE

Charley Hawse is Li'l Jinx's best frenemy and rival, as he is always playing pranks on the group. He teases Li'l Jinx often because he has a bit of a crush on her, but not as big as his crush on Gigi. Charley has quite the appetite on him (one that rivals that of Jughead's!) He may play baseball with the rest of the kids, but Charley absolutely loves football.

GREG

Greg might not be the strongest or the fastest kid on the block, but he loves playing sports with his friends. Both of his moms are athletic, which is where Greg gets his competitive spirit! Greg is a little bit of a show off, but he just wants to impress his friends. Greg also teases Li'l Jinx, but in a more playful way than Charley.

MORT

"Mort the worry wart" believes that if something can go wrong, it will go wrong, so he always keeps his expectations for himself low. Mort is easily scared, and often gets stomach aches when confronted with his fears. Mort's fears include heights, clowns, snakes, spiders, cats, cows, squirrels, birds, being alone, the doctor, the dark, flying… he's even scared of his own shadow! But what is Mort's #1 phobia? Phobophobia! The fear of fears!

GIGI

Gigi has been friends with Li'l Jinx for as long as she can remember, even before she became a popular child star. It's possible Gigi wouldn't be included in the friend group without her connection to Li'l Jinx, because the other kids think of her as stuck up. But Gigi has trouble interacting with kids her own age since she is always traveling for her acting roles. Gigi appeared in numerous television commercials, and Broadway shows, before finding mainstream fame with the TV show *We Love Sassy*. Gigi might be a little spoiled, but she always tries to share her wealth with her friends.

ROZ

Roz is the most level headed of the friend group, but she often misses out on the action, as her various after school activities keep her busy. Roz is extremely optimistic, and is always trying to learn new skills. She is a bit of an artist, and enjoys painting the most!

RUSS

Russel enjoys being the center of attention, but by no means is he self-absorbed. He just likes playing the class clown. He enjoys making his friends laugh with his jokes and drawings. But Russ is not always energetic, sometimes he likes to slow down and go stargazing.

HAP HOLLIDAY

Hap Holliday might seem like a temperamental father, when he butts heads with his daughter, but he loves her more than anyone else. That doesn't mean he'll let her get away with her shenanigans! While Hap enjoys playing with his daughter, he can sometimes take things over, causing further frustration. Hap tends to stress himself out, so he likes to take a break from his hectic life to relax and play golf. He may have trouble relating to his daughter, but after his divorce, Hap starts to become more overprotective, as he doesn't want to lose Li'l Jinx too.

MERY HOLLIDAY

Mery Holliday may seem absent from her daughter's life, but that's because her job as a nurse keeps her busy. Li'l Jinx's parents decided it was best for their daughter to live with Hap, as Mery's hectic schedule keeps her at the ER most of the time. Li'l Jinx may live with her father, but Mery often comes over to bake with her daughter. Mery was once an incredible softball player, and it seems she passed down her athletic abilities to her daughter. Mery and her girlfriend Mari always try their best to attend Li'l Jinx's little league games.

WELCOME TO COSMO!

Cosmo is the adventurous, quick-witted captain of his Martian crew. Together, they travel space in search of adventure and to help those in need! Cosmo's strength and leadership are tested as the villainous forces of Venus threaten the universe, as well as the thing Cosmo treasures most: his friends! In order to protect them, the Mighty Martian will have to seek out ancient treasures, battle monstrous mutants and go beyond brave as he ventures across the galaxy!

First Appearance:
Cosmo the Merry Martian #1, September 1958

Hair: Black

Eyes: Black

Hobbies: Seeking out new planets, helping those in need, playing pranks

Likes: Adventuring with friends, jokes, indie rock, BBQ sauce

Dislikes: Evildoers, wrinkled apparel, honey mustard

The adventure-hungry captain from Mars. Swashbuckling and confident, he can find a way out of any jam. Given he leads a crew of eccentric shipmates, Cosmo is bailing them out of danger more often than not!

DID YOU KNOW?

- Cosmo has a secret ability that allows him to see visions of the future, although the details are sometimes hard to make out.

ORBI

First Appearance:
Cosmo the Merry Martian #1, September 1958

Orbi is Cosmo's best friend. While he wants to be a hero like Cosmo and talks a big talk, he doesn't have the nerves to back it up. To his credit, he's always willing to lend a hand and can usually get himself out of danger with enough frantic flailing.

JOJO

First Appearance:
Cosmo the Merry Martian #1, September 1958

Jojo is Orbi's pet "dog" with metamorphic abilities. Often coming across as gruff and disinterested, he's obviously intelligent enough to interact with the crew. In secret, he is an ancient and nomadic hero–a legend among his people.

ASTRA

First Appearance:
Cosmo the Merry Martian #1, September 1958

Astra is the crew's pilot and wild card. She's eager to take on challenges–even unreasonable ones–but never purposefully at the expense of the crew.

She has a running romantic rivalry with Cosmo; they're both somewhat interested, but it's more fun to one-up each other.

MEDULLA

First Appearance:
Cosmo #1,
February 2018

A bright yet eccentric Martian scientist who is also considered to be the "gadget gal" of the group. A touch older than the others, but no less adventurous, Medulla exploits Cosmo and the crew's various adventures as a means of testing out her new inventions.

MAX STRONGJAW

First Appearance:
Cosmo #1,
February 2018

A human astronaut from the near-future. He was sent out to explore Mars in search for signs of life. Instead, Cosmo found (and rescued) him. Arrogant and out of his depth, Max tries to take command at all the wrong times. When push comes to shove, Max is a team player when it matters most.

PROFESSOR THIMK

First Appearance:
Cosmo the Merry Martian #1, September 1958

Professor Thimk is the self-proclaimed smartest man on Mars! He's joined on many of Cosmo's adventures and has used his intellect to get the crew out of many jams, even once saving Cosmo from the Venus Queen!

DR. BEATNIK

First Appearance:
Cosmo the Merry Martian #6, October 1959

Dr. Beatnik is a resident of Mars, though he certainly is not a member of Cosmo's crew. An unruly older Martian, Beatnik once plotted the invasion of Earth because he was fearful that Earthlings would bring their own culture like TV Westerns and Rock and Roll to Mars. Fortunately his invasion was defeated by team Cosmo and he hasn't tired it again... yet!

HESPER

First Appearance: *Cosmo* #1, February 2018

Hair: Hot pink

Eyes: Red

Hobbies: Taking over planets and turning it's inhabitants into her mindless slaves

Likes: Cosmo, beauty, power, hair spray, dark chocolate

Dislikes: Deception, failure, snow, sweet caramel

Hesper is the beautiful and tyrannical ruler of Venus. She commands her Battle Princesses and an army of monsters in a bid to conquer the solar system. They use the mineral Aphrodite to mutate their victims and add them to their army.

Before her time as Queen, Hesper and Cosmo shared a past. While the details are still a mystery, it is clear that she still greatly admires Cosmo despite his meddling with her plans.

BOUDICA

First Appearance:
Cosmo The Mighty Martian #3, January 2020

The newest and youngest of all the Battle Princesses, Boudica is determined to prove herself to Queen Hesper that she is a capable warrior.

Although sometimes teased by her peers for her naiveté and tender-heartedness, Boudica remains loyal to Venus. As a skilled swordswoman, she will slice down any opponents that challenge her home.

CLEO

First Appearance:
Cosmo #2,
March 2018

Cleo was the first of her peers to receive the title of Battle Princess from Queen Hesper. Studious and well-trained in close combat, the Venusian warrior uses her intellect to make quick decisions in battle.

After being defeated by Cosmo on Earth's moon, Cleo has vowed revenge against the mighty Martian for sullying her name and distrupting Hesper's grand plans.

SHIH

First Appearance:
Cosmo #5,
July 2018

A fierce warrior and highly competitive gamer, Shih utilizes her high-tech gear to pwn all challengers! Shih takes pride in utilizing the most state-of-the-art gadgets and will openly mock any n00bz who aren't on her level.

In addition to having all the gadgets, Shih is also the captain of the Red Flag, a Venusian ship with sails that are solar-powered!

WELCOME TO...
EVERYONE ELSE!

Archie and friends have been running around Riverdale for 80+ years, and have made numerous friends along the way! Some of these characters are from comics that predate Archie himself!

Archie Comics Publications (Originally known as MLJ) have been around since 1939, but Archie didn't even come into the picture until 1941!

Not every series became as popular as Archie, Josie and the Pussycats, Sabrina the Teenage Witch, or even Katy Keene. There have been other leading teens like Bingo Wilkin (no relation to Wilbur), Ginger Snapp, Suzie, Seymour, and Wilbur Wilkin (no relation to Bingo). There have been kooky animal characters like Super Duck, Cubby the Bear, Squoimy the Worm, and Bumbie the Bee-tective. There has been a Madhouse of characters like Captain Sprocket, Lester Square, and Chester Cool. Let's explore the World of Archie and meet the Pals and Gals who have been entertaining alongside the Riverdale gang for decades!

BINGO WILKIN

Woodrow "Bingo" Wilkin III, is a redheaded clumsy teenager from Midvale. Bingo is very similar to one Archie Andrews, but unlike Archie he is in a steady relationship with his next-door neighbor Samantha Smythe (much to her father's dismay!). His father often argues with Samantha's dad, Sampson, who tends to take his frustrations out on Bingo himself. The couple doesn't bother trying to hide their relationship from Sampson, but they do tend to move things over to Bingo's house when Samantha's father gets angry. While Samantha is physically much stronger than Bingo, he still tries to impress her with his strength (Although he almost always fails to do so). Bingo plays football for his school, and is the lead guitarist and singer for His band "The Bingoes," which he started with Samantha and their friends Teddy and Buddy. Bingo has a dog named Rebel, who often stops Teddy's plans to meddle in Bingo and Samantha's relationship. Teddy is the only one who is aware of just how smart Rebel actually is. Bingo's cousin is none other than Jughead Jones! The cousins might not see each other often, but when they do, they are the best of friends (maybe that's because Bingo is so similar to Juggie's actual best friend!)

WOODROW WILKIN II

While Woodrow "Willie" Wilkin II, has no issue with Bingo's girlfriend Samantha, he cannot stand her father Sampson. While he is not the one to start the arguments, Willie gets very frustrated with his neighbor, and lets him easily rile him up. He is prone to outbursts of anger and frustration, especially when Sampson refers to him as "Wee Willie Wilkins" (It's just Wilkin! There's no S!)

WILMA WILKIN

When her husband Willie gets frustrated, Wilma is always there to calm him down. Wilma enjoys spending time with her family, and she often invites her brother Herman over to spend time with her son Bingo. (She also tries to get her sister Gladys to stop by with her son Jughead, but they have to drive in from Riverdale, meanwhile Herman practically lives with the Wilkin family!) Wilma is best friends with Sheila Smythe, but they often have to hide their friendship so as to not upset their husbands further.

SAMANTHA SMYTHE

Samantha grew up living next door to Bingo Wilkin, so it made complete sense when the two teens started  dating. Sam just wants peace between the two families, but will not hide her feelings for Bingo from her father. Samantha enjoys weightlifting, and has been training with her father since she was a little girl. She is incredibly strong for her size and is very athletic, as she also dabbles in gymnastics.

SAMPSON SMYTHE

No one is quite sure how the feud between the Wilkins and the Smythes started, but Sampson is almost always the provoker. He often leans onto the Wilkin family fence to aggravate Willie, as he makes himself an easy target. While Sampson doesn't like Bingo, he knows deep down that he's good to his daughter.

SHEILA SMYTHE

It is Sheila's level headedness that balances her husband's temperament, but when all else fails  Sheila knows how to put Sampson in his place. She is the only one who can attempt to get her grouchy husband to see things from the point of view. Sheila and Wilma are happy that their children are dating, as they know they raised them right.

TEDDY TAMBOURINE

The "Mastermind of Mischief" Teddy is Bingo's frenemy who attempts to pursue Samantha's affection, but never  succeeds. He is immature and always scheming in an attempt to get Bingo out of the picture.

BUDDY DRUMHEAD

Buddy is Bingo's best friend. Buddy carries around a pair of drumsticks, and uses them wherever he goes. Without a pair of drumsticks in his hand, he doesn't know what to do with himself.

ZELDA MAXSON

Teddy sends Bingo to Zelda in an attempt to steal Samantha's away from him. But as it turns out Zelda is already aware of Bingo and Sam's relationship, and uses the opportunity to have Bingo introduce her to Buddy.

DIMPLES DELUSH

The seductive Dimples Delush will never turn down a dare. When Teddy uses her to come between Bingo and Samantha, (this seems to be a recurring theme…) Mr. Smythe steps in to stop her. As much as Sampson dislikes Bingo, he doesn't want to see his little girl heartbroken.

REBEL

Rebel is Bingo's faithful companion. He may be a small dog, but he can hold his own and is happy to defend Bingo if he needs to. Rebel may not speak aloud, but his thoughts are always made known some way or another!

NOELLE CLAUS

Noelle Claus is the teenage daughter of the one and only Santa Claus! When Noelle first visits Riverdale, she's a little distant, but that's because she's used to being isolated at the North Pole, and has never had friends her own age. All Noelle wants is to be treated like a regular teenager, which is why she gets along so well with Betty and Veronica.

JINGLES THE ELF

Jingles is "Santa's Best Brownie," who comes to visit Archie and friends every year around the holidays. The little eavesdropper often appears without warning and is prone to mischief, but he's not out to cause any harm. He has a job to do, and might as well have some fun with it.

SUGARPLUM

Sugarplum is a Christmas fairy from the North Pole. She also visits her Riverdale friends around the holidays, but her job is to spread Christmas cheer. Sugarplum can be clumsy and chaotic but her heart is in the right place. Jingles and Sugarplum have always had a playful rivalry, but when they are both disguised as humans named Jimmy and Summer, they fall in love, and have been in a relationship ever since.

TRICK

First Appearance:
Archie Halloween Spectacular, October 2022

A devious little imp with shape shifting abilities, Trick embraces the scarier side of Halloween and loves playing pranks on the unknowing residents of Riverdale! Trick shares a competitive streak with his fellow spirit, Treat, and will even team up with the likes of Reggie Mantle to ensure the scare factor wins over the sweet!

TREAT

First Appearance:
Archie Halloween Spectacular, October 2022

This spirit of Halloween loves all things sweet! Treat is all about good and spooky fun on Halloween, but most of all, Treat loves candy! Just as competitive as his fellow spirit Trick, Treat will assist the locals whose costumes are lackluster in hopes that fun will prevail and result in a huge candy haul by the night's end!

GINGER SNAPP

Ginger Snapp is the most popular girl in school! At least with the boys, that is! Ginger has a very active dating life, but she doesn't have "a type." She's dated all sorts of guys, from jocks, to straight-A students, shy boys, nerdy boys, rebels, etc. From the outside, Ginger may come across as superficial, as she puts a lot of time and effort into her appearance, but she's quite the opposite. Ginger never judges a book by its cover, and tends to be attracted to one's personality rather than their looks.

While Ginger has never fallen for a specific boy, there's something about Ickky that she likes, much to the bewilderment of her peers. Ginger has a shopping habit, and often spends too much of her father's income on new clothes. She doesn't like to wear the same outfit twice, and instead thinks of new ways to repeating wearing a piece with something new. Despite being raised primarily by her father, Ginger is extremely feminine and is quite crafty when it comes to coming up with ways to use her good looks to get dates, not that she has to try hard at all! She often dates the same guys as the equally attractive Bunny, but unlike Bunny, Ginger has a great personality to compliment her beauty.

DOTTIE

Dottie (later known as "Patsy") is Ginger's best friend and closest confidant. When Ginger has a crush, Dottie is the first to know, although she usually doesn't see what is so appealing to Ginger about these guys. Dottie is much pickier about her own dates, but for her that's a good thing. She'd rather wait for the right guy than date a bunch of boys she doesn't care much about.

ICKKY

His buddies are often confused how he can date a girl like Ginger, but Ickky's confidence might be his most attractive quality. However, their relationship isn't perfect, as Ickky takes Ginger for granted, before realizing how much he truly likes her. Ickky is thin and short for his age, and Ginger towers over him by quite a bit. But she is never embarrassed to be seen with him, and likes the attention he gives her. Ickky always feels the need to be right, and is awfully stubborn, which Ginger finds the most unappealing.

TOMMY TURNER

Tommy Turner is the only boy that Ginger is unable to "steal away" from Bunny, but when he sees how manipulative Bunny can be, he begins to like Ginger instead. Tommy is the complete opposite of Ickky, as he is tall, blonde, and muscular, which leads Ickky to see him as a rival for Ginger's affection.

SUZIE

Some might consider Suzie to be a bit ditzy, but she's also one of the sweetest girls you'll ever meet! While she may make mistakes, she remains cheerful and keeps moving forward! Suzie likes to try new things, as she is trying to discover what it is she wants to do with the rest of her life since graduating high school. But Suzie doesn't have as much free time as you might think. She fills up her schedule with all sorts of different activities, and always makes sure she leaves some time for volunteering, and helping out the less fortunate.

Although she has struggled to find her footing as an adult, Suzie remains optimistic. While her family and friends love her, they often try to avoid her help, as Suzie is quite the klutz and causes more trouble than it's worth. There is nothing that Suzie loves more than being outside and enjoying the fresh air. When she's not looking for a job, Suzie often spends her time working on her Uncle Jake's farm, or tending to her garden. As it turns out, Suzie has quite the green thumb!

FERDIE

While they're not exclusive, Suzie has been dating Ferdie for quite some time now. Ferdie knows Suzie is the only girl for him, and gets jealous whenever other guys hit on her. Ferdie is broke, and feels that he cannot afford to date a girl like Suzie, because all he can offer her is his love. But Suzie has been reluctant to commit to Ferdie, as he fails to take things seriously and is quite a slacker. Ferdie lives with his Uncle Blunderbuss, who acts as an uncle to all of his nephew's friends.

ANGELA THE ANGEL

Any time Suzie's niece Angela comes to visit, mischief ensues. She may appear sweet and innocent on the outside, but Angela is actively plotting against Suzie and her friends, as they are often the victims of her pranks. She has been deemed "Angela the Angel" as a nickname, but she is anything but!

GREGORY VON DRIPP

Gregory Von Dripp is friends with both Suzie and Ferdie, but has been known to date Suzie every now and then. Gregory is everything Ferdie is not. A well-spoken, put together, wealthy young man who already has a plan for his life. He might be vain, but Gregory is attracted to Suzie because of her positive attitude towards life.

WILBUR WILKIN

Wilbur Wilkin seems to live a parallel life to Archie Andrews! Though Wilbur actually pre-dates his red-headed contemporary. In fact, he made his first appearance in *Zip Comics* #18, three months before Archie's first appearance! Just like Archie with Betty and Veronica, Wilbur is in his own love triangle with the blonde Laurie Lake, and the brunette Linda Moore. But unlike Archie, Wilbur goes for the more pleasant Laurie than the self-absorbed Linda. This might be because Laurie balances Wilbur out more, as he can be quite conceited himself. But this devious teen still has good intentions… at least most of the time!

RED WILSON

If Wilbur Wilkin is Archie Andrews, then Red is his Jughead. Wilbur's best friend is known for his laziness and extreme appetite. Red often tries to freeload off his buddy, coming over to Wilbur's house to enjoy his snacks and amenities. While the rest of his friends spend their time competing over girls, Red never gets involved with the dating scene, as he enjoys watching his friends make fools of themselves.

SLATS MORGAN

When it comes to girls, Wilbur has had several rivals, but none have been as persistent as Slats, who wants Laurie all to himself. Unfortunately for both Wilbur and Slats, Laurie finds neither one of them attractive when they lose their temper with one another and start fighting. Surprisingly enough, when they aren't fighting over girls, Wilbur and Slats can be good friends just like Archie and Reggie! Woah! Wilbur really is living Archie's life!

LAURIE LAKE

The sweet Laurie Lake tries her best to keep her boyfriend Wilbur out of trouble, but is too apprehensive to get involved in his silly high jinks. While Laurie loves her boyfriend, she often tires of his antics, and wishes he would solve his problems in a more mature way.

LINDA MOORE

Linda Moore is dead set on breaking up Wilbur and Laurie's relationship, as she believes that she is more entitled to Wilbur's affection. She often schemes with her close friend and confidant Alec to figure out how to obtain Wilbur's attention. While it is no secret that Wilbur finds Linda attractive, he still seems to like Laurie more. But that's ok! Wilbur and Linda are probably too similar to work out anyhow!

DOTTY AND DITTO

Dotty is a cute little cowgirl, who lives on the "Wild 'n' Rowdy Ranch" with her grandfather. But her closest companion is her pet parrot Ditto, who rarely leaves her side. She often leaves the ranch to visit her boyfriend Dottum, who she enjoys fishing with. Dotty is very ambitious and courageous, but finds herself in some less-than-ideal situations, as she is often underestimated by adults.

PAT THE BRAT

For as long as his parents Alice and Oswald Smith can remember, Pat has always been a handful! Pat is simply smarter than other kids his age, and knows how to use his adorable looks to his advantage. When he's not causing trouble for his parents, Pat is either skateboarding or playing with his best friend Blinky and dog Fleabite.

SHRIMPY

Shrimpy is always outside playing with his best buddies Daphne, Brando, and Peggy, although Shrimpy and Daphne are always bickering. Peggy has a crush on Pipsqueak, but he's too oblivious to notice, and gets distracted very easily.

PIPSQUEAK

Pipsqueak might be too ambitious for his own good, as he is constantly getting himself in trouble with his dog, Pooch. Luckily for Pipsqueak, his parents are always there to clean up his mess!

Clyde Didit was known for hanging around Josie McCoy and friends long before her days as a Pussycat. Back then Clyde was unrecognizable! With his ginger perm and wild getups that always included his signature sunglasses and sandals, Clyde would walk around playing his sitar and singing folk music. Maybe he was inspired after watching Josie's rise to fame, or maybe he was tired of Pepper's constant teasing, but Clyde drastically changed his look after high school and created "The Madhouse Glads" with his younger brothers Dan, Dick, and Dippy. Long gone is Clyde's sunglasses and ginger perm! He now sports jet-black hair and is up to date with modern fashion trends. (Nobody outside of his family knows which is his natural hair color!).

While Clyde was very goofy in his younger days, he matured nicely into a great leader, and role model for his siblings. The Didit brothers can all play the same instruments, and tend to swap roles depending on the gig, but Clyde is almost always the lead vocalist of the group.

DAN DIDIT

Dan and Dippy Didit are actually twins! Danny strives to stand out from his brother by creating his own signature look. He is known for his tall, outlandish hats and bright, bold shirts. In fact, he somewhat resembles his brother Clyde from his folksinger days. (But maybe it's just the sunglasses…). Just like his brother, he outgrows this when he realizes that his bright blond hair is enough to discern him from Dippy, whose hair is more of a dirty blonde. Dan has a sweet tooth, and can be spotted snacking on desserts backstage.

DICK DIDIT

The redheaded Richard Didit is the youngest Didit sibling. Dick is somewhat of a worrywart who is always thinking about the future of the band. He would feel responsible if the Glads failed, because he is the songwriter of the group.

DIPPY DIDIT

When The Madhouse Glads first became popular, Dippy Didit decided to use his fame for good, speaking on social issues, attending protests, and encouraging his young fans to get more involved in politics. He was the first in the group to realize their fans would listen to what they had to say, and wanted to be a good influence.

FRAN THE FAN

Fran is the ultimate fangirl, who met The Madhouse Glads in their early days as a band. After noticing her at a few performances, Clyde joked that she must be their number one fan, and Fran decided to take the role very seriously! Fran followed them around to every gig they got until they became close enough to invite her to join them on their ventures. Fran is a nice girl, but is a little too energetic for the laid-back style of The Madhouse Glads. While Fran likes all of the Didit siblings, it is Clyde and Danny who she tends to date the most.

ROD THE MOD

Rod Roman is extremely self-absorbed, and believes that he is doing The Madhouse Glads a favor by hanging around them so often. Why he does spend so much time with the Glads is unknown, but it is speculated that he likes any attention, even negative attention! Rod and Fran dated for a little bit, but after constantly remarking to Fran that he's out of her league, she ended things, and now Rod constantly tries to distract her attention away from the Glads.

Seymour was once his father's pride and joy, but now that he has grown up into a typical teenager boy, his father has a hard time understanding him. Seymour tries his best, but still can't help but think he is constantly disappointing his Poppa. He tries to spend most of his free time enjoying life rather than focusing on homework or his chores, which further frustrates his Pops. Seymour is very resourceful and often finds a more creative solution when it comes to completing such mundane tasks. Seymour is popular amongst his peers and is often the life of the party, although he can also be borderline obnoxious. He stands out with the girls because of his flirty personality, and charming humor. (They also love his dimples!) His friends may tease him when they witness him flirting, but at least Seymour has the confidence to approach the girls he finds attractive.

YOUNG DR. MASTERS

The charming and handsome David Masters is anything but an ordinary doctor, he is constantly putting himself in danger to help others. His father is much more of a traditionalist who always dreamed of the two of them working together someday, as Old Dr. Masters and Young Dr. Masters. But his patients don't trust the young doctor, and fail to take him seriously because of his age and inability to give them an easy diagnosis.

David knows that general medicine is not for him, but is struggling to find his place in the medical world. David longs to spend more time in his medical lab, because he believes his scientific research could lead to a breakthrough in modern medicine. Something his father, and his fiancée Brenda Moore, fail to understand. Brenda is more in love with the idea of marrying a doctor and creating the perfect family, than she is with David.

The only person who supports David is nurse Sally Redmond, who he starts to develop feelings for! Despite his complicated love life, young Dr. Masters continues to brave the most alarming situations to help injured people who might not be able to make it to the hospital in time.

JAKE CHANG

One of the youngest detectives to enter Riverdale, Jake Chang has come to solve the mysteries surrounding Archie and his friends and will even team up with them to crack the case!

FU CHANG

The Chinese scholar and American educated detective Fu Chang, has dedicated his life to helping the oppressed and is devoted to the teachings of the Chinese Gods. Upon his death, Sing Po, a famous magician and direct descendant of Aladdin, leaves Chang a set of magic chessmen, who possess all the powers of Aladdin's lamp. Fu Chang uses the powers of Aladdin to organize the Ti Yan Tong, a secret society dedicated to taking down the evil sorceress Princess Ling Foy. It is Fu Chang's intelligence and skills that make him such a great leader.

TAY MING

Tay Ming is Fu Chang's fiancée and closest confidant who helps him organize the Ti Yan Tong. After defeating Princess Ling Foy, they hope to bring peace to the people of San Francisco's Chinatown, something easier said than done. Tay Ming often falls into the damsel in distress role, as she is often captured by Princess Ling Foy and her evil creations.

Sam Hill is an ex-Ivy League halfback and boxer turned crime fighter! He may appear as a clean-cut college professor, but Sam Hill Private Eye is a tough detective with a sharp tongue and advanced athletic abilities. The world around Hill resembles that of a gritty film noir with dangerous thugs, petty criminals, and sexy women. Although Sam tends to work alone without the help of the cops, who are not very fond of the tough talking detective, he sometimes teams up with police detective, Lt. Dugan, although the two generally distrust each other. Sam Hill is very confident and smooth-talking. He thinks the white streak in his hair makes him look distinguished (and many women will agree!). Sam has a soft spot for his secretary Roxanna, though the two don't often fraternize outside of work.

SUPER DUCK

Walter Webfoot becomes the high flying indestructible "Super Duck the Cock-eyed Wonder" after encountering magical crackers (quackers!). With his new powers acquired, Super Duck has no time for the foolishness of the villains he encounters in Ducktropolis. Eventually his friends and family find out about his secret identity and start referring to Walter as "Supe," despite crime being relatively dormant by that point.

Eventually the only fights Supe is involved in are the ones caused by his own irritable attitude. Supe is an extremely temperamental duck who wants to be left alone in his own peaceful world. He has a hard time putting up with his nephew's foolishness. While Supe himself is not necessarily a klutz, he seemingly always manages to hurt himself, which only irritates him further. Honestly, there's not a lot that doesn't annoy Super Duck, and anything could cause him to blow his lid!

Uwanna is Super Duck's girlfriend, who must be extremely tolerant to put up with Supe's poor behavior, although she might be the only person able to put him in his place. She is also known to lose her temper, but with the situations Supe creates, can you blame her?! She often comes home from work to find Supe expecting her to clean up whatever mess he created that day. But Uwanna is having none of that! Despite their arguments, Uwanna cares about her boyfriend very much, and tries to get him to be more reasonable.

FAUNTLEROY

Fauntleroy is Supe's troublesome nephew, who always has a new prank to try out on his uncle. Even when he is not playing a prank on his uncle, he is close by his side asking all sorts of questions and talking his ear off! (Do ducks have ears?) Fauntleroy is more optimistic than both Supe and Uwanna, and tries to spend his days having fun (Although, Fauntleroy's idea of fun frequently involves tricking Supe in some way).

KARDAK THE MYSTIC

The mystic sorcerer John Cardy goes by "Kardak the Mystic" to battle against those who use their magic talents for evil, especially the sinister magicians the Master Brahmins. His powers include hypnosis and invisibility, and he travels with his faithful servant Balthar. Kardak's only weakness is his love for his fiance Lorna.

BENTLEY OF SCOTLAND YARD

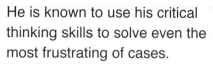

Inspector Bently of Scotland Yard frequently runs into paranormal entities that turn out to be some sort of a hoax. He is known to use his critical thinking skills to solve even the most frustrating of cases.

LEE SAMPSON

The loyal and hardworking Lee Sampson is a student at the naval academy whose special skills include rowing, and jiu jitsu. Sampson competes with his rival Don Lewis for the affections of the pilot Mae Dennis, who Sampson meets after saving her from a plane crash.

MIDSHIPMAN

Lee Sampson is a part of the midshipman, who often join Sampson on his crusades. Just like Sampson, these young men of the navy are trained to use their athletic abilities to help those in need.

MAD DOCTOR DOOM

The evil scientist Mad Doctor Doom desires to conquer the world, and control everyone on it. He develops his plans in a secret lab, located on the edge of Riverdale, in Crackstone Manor. There he builds all sorts of machines and inventions to assist in his plans, but is always stopped (often by accident) by Little Archie. When Mad Doctor Doom realizes he will always fail with Little Archie around, he invents the "Time Taxi," to attempt to take over the world before Little Archie is even born. Fortunately, the incompetent evil mastermind is still unable to take over Riverdale, much less the world, and decides to lay low for a while. Doctor Doom comes back as a nemesis to the Superteens, but it is unclear if he realizes Pureheart the Powerful is his old arch rival Little Archie.

CHESTER PLUNKETT

Chester Plunkett is Mad Doctor Doom's teenage assistant. Chester's lack of a parental figure growing up has led him to becoming attached to the evil scientist, and looks up to him as a father. Despite this, Mad Doctor Doom often takes him for granted. He might be a few grades ahead of Little Archie and friends, but Chester is a lot less intelligent and a lot more gullible.

DANNY IN WONDERLAND

After reading "Stories of the Land of Wonder" while visiting his Uncle's ranch, Danny makes a wish that leads him and his dog Snapper to be transported to the Land of Wonder from his book. It's there that Danny meets Kuppie who joins him on his adventure through Wonderland.

GLOOMY GUS

The homeless ghost Gus Gloompuss is looking for a new body to inhabit, but is having little to no success transferring his soul. Everytime Gloomy Gus thinks he's about to be human once more, something ultimately goes wrong. His spontaneous sidekick Gabby the angel tries to guide him with advice, but usually her guidance is not very helpful at all.

DICK STORM

Richard Storm is a top-notch adventurer, well known internationally for his courage, strength and intelligence. Dick's goal is to fight against the forces of tyranny and injustice and is never afraid to take charge and put himself in danger to do so. He is often recruited to go undercover on his quests all over the world.

CUBBY THE BEAR

The impulsive Cubby the Bear can be quite reckless when he doesn't think his actions through. He usually means well enough, until he runs into his rival Foxy, the forest tormentor, who always knows how to irritate Cubby. Cubby is afraid of heights and avoids them at all costs.

SQUOIMY THE WORM

Squoimy the Worm is a talking bookworm whose intelligence comes from the book that he jumped out of. He started writing his own poetry to impress his girlfriend Annabelle, but her affections are distracted by Squoimy's nemesis Moe Squito. But the hopeless romantic Squoimy will do anything he can to win her back.

BUMBIE THE BEE-TECTIVE

Bumbie the Bee-tective is Bugville's personal private eye. Bumbie is more intelligent than most of the town's inhabitants, as he has a mail ordered detective school degree. With his detective hat, and magnifying glass, Bumbie the Bee-tective is on the case!

CAPTAIN SPROCKET

The conceited and overconfident Captain
Sprocket is the last person you want help
from in an emergency, as his foolish antics
often get in his own way. The bumbling
superhero has a hard time finding the best
solution for the problem and instead tends to
do whatever will make him appear the most
competent. He broke up with his previous
girlfriend Thelma because he found her clingy
and annoying, but he is just as unappreciative
of his wife Gladys. His nephew looks up to
him more than anyone and dresses up in
his own version of his uncle's superhero
costume, but his admiration is seen as a
nuisance to Sprocket.

MIGHTY CHICK

Captain Sprocket may prefer to work alone,
but he does later admit to needing help when
he teams up with Mighty Chick. Mighty Chick
is the polar opposite to Sprocket in many
ways, as her greatest superpower is how
much she cares for those around her. Both
Sprocket and Mighty Chick have superhuman
strength but Mighty Chick doesn't like to be a
showoff.

SUPER SNAIL

Super Snail falls asleep during battle nearly every time, it's a wonder how he is always able to save the day! His laziness has led him to create all sorts of gadgets to do his hard work for him while he dozes off. Despite sleeping during most of them, Super Snail is exhausted after every fight!

CAPTAIN PUMPERNIK

Captain Pumpernik of the Royal Transylvanian Astrocorps takes flight in his spaceship in an attempt to be the first vampire on the moon! Despite his initial failures, Captain Pumpernik is extremely optimistic, and won't give up!

THE BLIPS

The Blips are curious little creatures from outer space who kinda resemble jelly beans (If jelly beans had arms and legs... and hair). The colorful Blips hide in plain sight in loud artwork, clothing, and even TV commercials to observe the humans of earth. They are careful not to expose themselves too often, as they cause the humans they interact with to run away screaming.

CAPTAIN COMMANDO

Naval Commander John Grayson takes the identity of "Captain Commando" to fight Nazis with the help of "The Boy Soldiers" a team comprised of Billy Grayson (John's son), Gerald Sykes, Armand De Latour, and Erik Jansen. While the young boys are from different parts of the world, they are brought together by their admiration of Captain Commando and their love of freedom. John hides his identity from his son in an attempt to protect him, but is afraid that his son is ashamed of him until Billy reveals that he knew his father's identity all along, and has immense respect for him.

CAPTAIN FLAG

Captain Flag is best known for his rivalry with "The Black Hand," a pale figure who strangles his victims to death till their skin turns a dark shade of charcoal. Wealthy playboy Tommy Townsend becomes Captain Flag after he watches The Black Hand murder his father, and almost himelf until he is saved by a large american eagle who he nicknames "Yank."

CAPTAIN VALOR

Adventurer Captain Valor retires from his position in the US Marine Corps because he didn't find the Marines fulfilling enough. Although he craves adventure, there's nothing more that he wants in life than to help those in need.

DOC REEVES

Doctor Malcom Reeves is known for accompanying the Mighty Crusaders when his intelligence is needed. He was given the nickname "Doc" as a child, and while he considers himself a man of science, he does not hold a doctorate. Doc feels the need to make himself useful, and does so by running and repairing the computers in the Crusaders hideout. He believes in what the Crusaders stand for, and exhausts his efforts trying to help them in any way he can.

GYPSY JOHNSON

The adventurer Gypsy Johnson, Texan soldier of fortune, is extremely observant and always follows his intuition. It's on his adventures that he meets Dorothy Collier and her brother Leonard who join him on his quests around the world.

HERCULES

Hercules "The Modern Champion of Justice," is the strongest man in history. After earning his place on Mt. Olympus, his father Zeus sent him back to the land of the mortals-Earth to clear the world of wrongdoers. While Hercules means well, he often stirs up trouble for himself as he has a hard time understanding modern society.

MARCO LOCO

While he would think more highly of himself, Marco Loco is an easily distracted stowaway, who voyages the sea with his best pal Snooch. While he is always finding himself in sticky situations, Marco is known to outsmart his captors.

PENNY PARKER

Society girl Penelope "Penny" Parker defies the snobbish lifestyle of her upper class parents. Penny would much rather spend her time at the gym practicing her punching with her boxing trainer Pug, who also functions as her closest confidant. After outsmarting a thief at her deb party, Penny decides to become a private detective.

POKEY OAKEY

The "funniest funny man of them all" Pokey Oakey has two main pleasures in life: eating and sleeping. Pokey lives  in Catfish creek with his parents and his little sister Butter Bean. While Catfish Creek is known to be a great place to forget your responsibilities and relax, Pokey is always unintentionally getting into trouble.

STACEY KNIGHT, M.D.

The young Stacey Knight, M.D. is often called on by the police to help on difficult cases, because of his  uncanny ability to solve crimes. Stacey often gets too involved with his work, and seems to spend more time injuring thugs than healing patients. Doctor Knight always gives criminals a taste of their own medicine.

FRAN FRAZER

News photographer Fran Frazer works for *Strife Magazine* and will never back down from danger if it means she can get a good shot! Fran bickers with rival newspaper reporter Hal Davis until the two realize that they'll both benefit if they work as a team, Hal will get the story, and Fran will get the photos. The two correspondents have a strong chemistry together, and when they think they're about to meet their demise, they reveal their true feelings for each other.

DOVER BOYS

The Dover brothers inherit their love for adventure from their parents, who disappeared on an expedition when the boys were just kids. Now the Dover Boys are raised by their Aunt Martha and Uncle Dan, who fuel the boys' adventurous spirit. 18-year-old Dan is the more serious brother, while 17-year-old Tim can be a bit too enthusiastic at times. But just like their parents, the Dover Boys are extremely resourceful when they find themselves in a dilemma. The Dover family has an enemy in the old town miser Silas Croombs, whose egocentric son Claude despises Dan and Tim. The brothers tag alongside their Uncle Bill to search for an ancient Inca treasure.

CHESTER COOL

The smooth talking "Chester the Hipster" knows how to get what he wants! His confidence can get him through any situation. He seems to not be afraid of anything, but fears Chester has are hidden behind his sunglasses. Chester is popular with the ladies, as it seems he always knows the right thing to say. Chester loves attention, whether positive or negative. Maybe that is why he is always messing with his best buddy Lester. While he might be manipulative at times, Chester is still a loyal friend and makes sure that everyone knows he is the only one allowed to mess with Lester.

LESTER SQUARE

The block headed Lester Square is much more insecure and nerdy than his buddy Chester. While Chester doesn't put much effort into anything but himself, Lester is always trying too hard to overcompensate for his lack of confidence. But Lester still is popular with the ladies, as some girls think his nervous behavior is adorable. But when the two friends are not out on dates, Les and Ches are almost always hanging out together.

SERGEANT BOYLE

After his ship back home to America is sunk by a German sub, Sergeant Boyle devotes his attention to fighting in World War 2. His athletic ability and need for action aid Sergeant Boyle as he travels with his partner Captain Twerp to fight for justice.

RANG A TANG THE WONDER DOG

Rang a Tang the Wonder Dog exhibits more heroic characteristics than most humans! Rang a Tang exudes amazing athletic abilities and is not afraid to throw himself in harm's way. While he might be a dog, his intelligence is apparent to anyone he encounters. Rang a Tang becomes loyal to detective Hy Speed, after saving his life during a chase.

CATFISH JOE

Catfish Joe is a dimwitted young man from the Mississippi swamplands. He's a simple boy, who is easily tricked into doing things for his neighbors who take advantage of poor Joe. But Joe doesn't mind helping others at all, he has a strong heart and loves his mother Mammy and his girlfriend Maybelle more than anything else.

SEE YOU AGAIN SOON!

We hope you enjoyed this tour of Riverdale! But with over 80 years of content and thousands of people, places, and things, we may have missed a few notable names and faces. Did you spot anyone we may have forgotten? Anything else about the Archie Universe you'd like to know more about? Drop us a line at **fanart@archiecomics.com!**